The astonishing worlds of Piers Anthony...

THE MODE SERIES

Five friends from alternate worlds face love and danger across time and space.

"Fresh, imaginative." —*Publishers Weekly*

THE APPRENTICE ADEPT SERIES

The incredible story of one world inhabited by two spheres—the technology of Proton and the magic of Phaze...

"One of Anthony's most popular series." —*Library Journal*

KILLOBYTE

In this futureworld of virtual reality, the game is all too real—and if you lose, you die...

"Exhilarating!" —*Chicago Tribune*

MERCYCLE

The ingredients include one boy, one underwater bicycle, and a mermaid or two—instant adventure, just add water!

THE CATERPILLAR'S QUESTION

The first-time-ever collaboration by bestselling masters Piers Anthony and Philip Jose Farmer. The Imago, a powerful immortal spirit, is a young student's only hope against a tyrannical empire. But anyone and anything can be the Imago—even a mute, crippled human girl...

HARD SELL

Who'd be stupid enough to buy real estate on Mars? Meet Mr. Fisk Centers. Is he a hero or a sucker? You be the judge...

"Piers Anthony [is] always entertaining!" —*Rave Reviews*

Piers Anthony's bril[...] [...]es—a novel that explor[...] [...]g the time stream . . . an[...] [...]uman destiny.

ILLUSTRATIONS BY
PATRICK WOODROFFE

This Ace Book contains the complete text of the original trade edition. It has been completely reset in a typeface designed for easy reading, and was printed from new film.

BALOOK

An Ace Book / published by arrangement with
the author

PRINTING HISTORY
Underwood-Miller trade edition / 1990
Ace mass-market edition / January 1997

Cover art by Patrick Woodroffe.
Book design by Casey Hampton.

For information address: The Berkley Publishing Group,
200 Madison Avenue, New York, New York 10016.

The Putnam Berkley World Wide Web site address is
http://www.berkley.com/berkley

ISBN: 0-441-00398-2

ACE®
Ace Books are published by The Berkley Publishing Group,
200 Madison Avenue, New York, New York 10016.
ACE and the "A" design
are trademarks belonging to Charter Communications, Inc.

PRINTED IN THE UNITED STATES OF AMERICA

10 9 8 7 6 5 4 3 2

CONTENTS

ILLUSTRATIONS

The Trees beyond the fence were in poorer state

1 BREAKOUT

THOR NEMMEN CLIMBED the steps of the high stile and looked over the fence. The top strand was electrified, and was six meters above the ground—almost twenty feet in the old measure. That had once been a daunting height.

Thor always paused at this point, aware of his vulnerability. Today there was a moderate wind that tugged at his clothing, as if to nudge him off his perch. Nearby stood the pretty trees of the estate: small poplar, with the leaves shimmering; taller birch, with the white bark that looked as if it had been carelessly painted in horizontal swipes; and still taller pine, the seeming monarch of this forest. The whole region was growing up, now that all trees of all types were protected species, and it was good.

But the trees beyond the fence were in poorer state than those on the side from which he had come. They were relatively lean, their lower branches pruned well back. New growth was showing on some, but it would be long before their foliage was normal. Only above the level of about eight meters was it full.

"Balook!" he called. No point in climbing down inside, when he could ride instead.

There was no response. Concerned, Thor peered across the forest pasture. He hoped his huge friend wasn't sick. Ordinarily Balook came galloping eagerly, nose lifted, tail trailing, shaking the ground with his solid hooves. But this morning the landscape was vacant from pond to pines.

Quickly Thor swung himself over the top and trotted down the inner ramp. He jumped the last meter to the ground and ran along the fence toward the distant stable. "Balook!" he called again.

Half a kilometer along, he came across disaster. A tremendous hole had been ripped in the fence, as though a juggernaut had smashed through, two meters above the ground. The topmost cable was all that remained of the upper two-thirds of the barrier.

Thor stopped and stared, aghast at the damage. He had not believed that anything short of a runaway construction tractor could break that fence. That would have left treadmarks on the ground and taken out the bottom section, not the top. Anything except—

Then the significance of the break came to him. Suddenly he was running at top speed, shouting. "Balook! Balook's broken out!"

Breathless, he rushed up to the ranch house and pounded on the door. "Skip! Skip! Balook's gone!"

The guest-screen in the door lighted and the burly foreman's face appeared. "Shut up and make sense a minute!'' the face snapped, seeming gruffer than it was.

''Skip, Balook broke out!'' Thor cried.

The door sprang open, propelled by an imperative foot. The foreman ran his thumbnail along the crease of his plastic shirt, sealing it shut. Obviously he had been interrupted while getting dressed; his feet were bare, his thinning red hair tousled. ''Don't talk nonsense, lad! That fence is anchored by twenty-thousand-pound cable.''

Quickly Thor translated the man's old-fashioned measurement into familiar terms: twenty thousand pounds would be about nine thousand kilograms, or nine metric tons. ''How much does Balook weigh, now?''

''Nine tons,'' Skip said, spraying on temporary slippers. Then, as he waited a few seconds for the porous plastic to set, he did a doubletake. ''By jingo, lad, you're right! Balook *could* break out, if he had a mind to! I keep thinking of him as the little tyke he was when we started.'' Skip's tons were only nine tenths as big as Thor's, but hardly made a difference in this case. ''But why would he *want* to?''

Thor hadn't thought of it that way. Now he felt an unfamiliar lump in his throat. ''He *doesn't* want to! He likes it here!''

''And why no alarm? You say the fence is broken, and mind you, I'm not questioning your word, lad, but the current must have been interrupted, then. Are you *sure*—?''

''I'll show you the place,'' Thor said quickly. ''The power strands are still in place. He must have shied away from them.''

Skip followed him down to the fence. The break was in the forest section, so they had to get quite close before it was visible. Thor was perversely afraid it wouldn't be there, now that he had announced it, and that he'd be shown up for a fifteen year old wolf-crier. But then they saw it. "There!" he cried.

Skip inspected the break with professional competence. "He broke it, all right! The force was from the inside. Must've ducked his head and pulled up his feet and hurtled through. I should have known he was getting too big for this compound."

"But *why*?" Thor cried, seeing it as a personal betrayal. Then his lip curled, as he got a notion. "Someone must have been teasing him again—peppering him with buckshot—"

Skip reached across and tousled Thor's hair—an action Thor had never much liked, yet had not been able to protest. Their hair was the same color, but Thor's was much thicker. It seemed that this gave Skip a proprietary right. "You've been reading westerns again, lad. Citizens don't carry guns any more, remember? Not unless they're deputized for some emergency. Not since those assassinations of the Sixties and Seventies—"

"And Eighties and Nineties," Thor agreed. "I know. But Balook just *wouldn't* have done it on his own!"

Skip shook his head. "He's a big, big animal, lad. Largest hoofer ever. Twice the size of an elephant. Now he's filling out, maybe feeling his oats."

"Balook doesn't eat oats!"

Skip half-smiled. "Lots of males feel 'em that don't

eat 'em, lad. You will too, soon enough. We don't know what's going on in his long head."

"But he wouldn't leave me!"

Skip didn't answer directly. "Remember," he said grimly, "he's big, but he's not smart. He could be hurt or lost already—and it'll take at least two days to requisition a copter."

Thor's anger turned to apprehension for Balook, then back to anger. He was furious at this seemingly callous appraisal, for he loved Balook better than any person. But he was also angry at the animal for walking out on him in the night. It wasn't just the matter of breaking out; it was that Balook had gone *alone*, not waiting for Thor.

Gone where?

Skip looked at the tracks. The footprints were so heavy that the soft ground remained depressed, and the huge three toes showed separately. "No one forced him, looks like. See, lad—the spoor leads straight up to the break, and straight away from it. Little blood . . . and that's from the broken wires as he went through. He knew what he was doing, all right. He had somewhere to go." Then, before Thor could make another meaningless protest: "Come on, lad—we'd better have a huddle with the boss."

Thor followed the foreman, numb. How could Balook have done this? The huge, friendly animal had always sought Thor's company, and mourned when Thor was absent. Balook knew that Thor always came for a visit in the morning, and so he was always near the stile. To take off like this—it just didn't make sense!

They met with the Project Manager, Don Scale, in

his crowded office. Scale was in his fifties, and somewhat pudgy and short; he looked incompetent, but probably wasn't. Thor had never really gotten along with him.

Manuals and papers were piled up on the desk, and pictures of the Project layout were on the near wall. At one edge of a side table lay a portable self-powered lie detector that had always fascinated Thor. Its technical name was complex and irrelevant, and it wasn't intended as a security measure anyway. Every day Scale used it to take a reading on Balook, to determine the animal's overall state of health and tension; if Balook was nervous or in minor pain, the needle swung off the TRUE marker toward FALSE. The stronger the upset, the farther over the needle went.

Thor smiled to himself. There were years' worth of readings in the Project files, but they were meaningless. Balook did not like Scale and was always tense when the man came near. When Scale had been away for some conference, Skip took the readings—and they were much different, much closer to TRUE. Scale was in effect taking his own pulse. Somehow the man had never quite caught on to that.

Skip quickly filled Scale in. "No sign of foul play," he finished. "Must've wanted to get out and explore the neighborhood."

"And maybe that curiosity will kill him!" Scale snapped. "He must be recovered at all costs!"

"He may not want to *be* recovered," Skip said. "He's basically a wild animal, come of age—"

"He's tame!" Thor cried.

"Tame around *you*, Nemmen," Scale said. He always used Thor's surname, which was one of the reasons Thor disliked him. Scale had never approved of Thor's participation in the Project, and seemed to be constantly trying to depersonalize him. "Less so around the rest of us. And as for strangers—"

"He's wary of them," Thor agreed. "But any animal would be. Especially when they tend to see him as a freak."

"There is a tremendous amount of money and skill invested in this project," Scale said. "The beast is unique. We must take all feasible steps—"

"Money!" Thor cried contemptuously. There was yet another thing about the man that annoyed him: his preoccupation with money. To him Balook was not a living creature so much as an investment. Beast, indeed!

"Listen, young man!" Scale said sharply, for once forgetting the surname as his fat jowl tightened. "You're only here on sufferance—"

Skip put a cautioning hand on Scale's arm. "Easy, boss. The lad's got as much invested as anybody, only not in Caesar's coin. And he's the only one of us Balook really trusts."

Scale grudgingly calmed himself. "Still, he ought to appreciate the gravity of the situation. If that animal kills one human being—"

"Balook would never harm a person!" Thor cried. He had to fight back unmanly tears at the notion of such a charge. He could debate an issue about any other animal with vigor, but Balook was special. "He's gentle and shy—"

"He's a rhinoceros," Scale said. "Rhinos are ornery—especially the big ones. He could turn ugly."

"Not intentionally," Skip said, answering compassionately. "I've got to agree with the lad, sir—Balook is basically gentle." He returned to Thor. "But his sight is weak, especially in daylight. And he's big, mighty big. The way he broke that fence—well, he'd be hard put to it to stop in time, if he saw a man in the way. If he stampeded—"

Thor put his face in his hands. He knew that Balook *could* stampede, and in that state crush anything in his path. Then he would have to be killed, for that was the law. Visitors were warned away from the ranch, nominally for their own protection, but actually for Balook's. Now Balook was loose in human territory; all bets were off.

"The money is extremely close," the Manager said. "If we lose Balook, it will be all over for the Project."

To that much Thor could agree wholeheartedly, though without gaining any respect for Scale.

The men continued to discuss pros and cons in practical terms. Thor was unable to keep his mind on such things. Balook was gone!

He remembered how he had first met Balook, back when the Project had first taken over this forest ranch. He had been a child of nine then, a neighbor's boy with time on his hands and boundless curiosity. He had never gotten along well with children his own age, so was alone much of the time.

Unlike some loners, he was lonely. He had craved companionship, but not really of the human kind. His pet pony had foundered and been put away, making it worse. He had related to that animal better than to any

It was grotesque, even for a rhino

human being. He had learned early that he could not afford to be open about his attachment, because others simply did not regard such a thing as significant. An animal dead? Too bad, and get another as good or better than the first. It was a nice animal? Surely so—but it was after all only a horse. Now stop whining and do your homework.

So he had wandered alone. The fence around the compound had not been as high and strong then, and the grounds had remained in a state of natural wildness, rather than the cultivated wilderness of contemporary fashion. It had been easy for a child to sneak in and poke about.

He had been amazed to discover a small zoo. Several female rhinoceroses were penned in what was now the tremendous stable. They were not particularly friendly, and though their noses had been de-horned they remained dangerous brutes. He stayed clear of them.

But one was different. It was naturally hornless, and skinny and young—a year or less. It weighed several times as much as the boy, but was obviously a baby. It was grotesque even for a rhino, yet also cute in the manner of any young animal. In fact, it could be thought to resemble a deformed pony. And it was lonely.

Thor had not realized just how remarkable that ungainly calf was. It nursed on the mother rhinos, who tolerated it only because they were confined and drugged, but it was of a different species. None of them could have birthed it naturally; none would lick it or comfort it, this homely pseudo-rhino. This ugly duckling creature.

The thing was miserable. Men took care of it, cleaned its pen, washed its body, inoculated it, exercised it, protected it . . . and the rest of the time it stood in its isolated pen and bawled until it slept.

Thor recognized the tone; he had often felt that way himself. The calf was emotionally isolated. When Thor extended his hand to it through the slats, it had first shied away in fright, then come close to sniff and lick eagerly, making little sounds of gratification. It seemed that no one had come to it before, just for company.

All it needed was a friend.

Thor had a similar need.

They had become associates, surreptitiously. Thor would hide until the keepers went to the back shed for private beer and poker. Then he would join Balook, petting the calf, talking to him, brushing down his soft fur, being his friend. The calf was comforted, and so was the boy.

It was, really, the only friendship either party had, that asked for nothing in return except acceptance and companionship.

But Thor got careless, after several weeks, and did not allow for random variations in the Project schedules. One of the men caught him in the pen. Don Scale was summoned. The Project Manager was appalled that his invaluable charge was subject to the intrusions of a neighborhood brat. He reprimanded the boy severely and banned him from the premises.

It was a blow to Thor, for there now seemed to be no use for his life. The long happy hours in the warm stable had given meaning to his existence. Without Balook there was nothing.

Balook, too, languished. He was five hundred kilograms of helplessness, bawling plaintively in his pen. After a few days he gave up and lay there whimpering, lacking the initiative even to feed. The joy of companionship he had learned was now cruelly denied, and he had no way to understand. The lie-detector needle remained steadily on FALSE, confirming that Balook was really in trouble.

Don Scale was not a stupid man, or an unduly arrogant one. He recognized the situation and resolved to make the lesser evil of it. Young Thor Nemmen received a formal pass and was added to the payroll at a nominal rate, with the title "Companion."

That had been six years ago. Ever since, Thor had visited Balook daily, playing with him, climbing all over him, sharing his food in a fashion, snoozing with him. The animal had grown enormously, even after allowing for his nature; Scale's charts showed above-projected gains. Thor taught the rhino how to heed his directions when he rode, so they could share more fun by exploring the compound. Balook was never allowed to run loose within the "business" section of the Project, but when he was with Thor it didn't count. Balook was no genius, even for a rhino, but he was quick enough to learn that he had greater freedom when playing Thor's game than he did otherwise. Besides, exploring was fun. There were green growing trees out there, his favorite food after he was weaned from milk.

During school season they had to make special arrangements, for Balook could not understand the reason for Thor's absences. Thus Thor was permitted to attend TV classes—with the set in Balook's pen. This was an unforeseen blessing, for though Thor was willing to learn anything, he hated being crammed into a classroom with his peers. Boys his age tended to be loutish. They respected only those who had the muscle or skill to knock heads, and Thor was of barely average physical stature and had indifferent coordination. Some few boys had the compensation of intellect; Thor was not competitive there either. As a person he was rated at sixes and sevens; nobody found him worthwhile. Balook had freed him of that. To Balook, he was the greatest person in the world.

The animal seemed to enjoy the programs, too, though he could hardly have understood them. Probably it was merely the rhino's feeling of participation with his friend that gave him pleasure. Once Thor had dreamed that he had dropped in on Balook unexpectedly, and caught him doing differential equations with his hoof in the dirt while the TV had a college math class on. 'I didn't know you could do that!' he exclaimed. 'Well, you never asked,' Balook replied. Then Thor had caught on, and woke up laughing. It was a foolish dream; Balook was the most remarkable creature on earth as he stood; he didn't need to be a genius too.

Once Balook had fallen ill, despite the precautions of expensive veterinarians. Thor had to make special arrangements to stay with him day and night; the animal had little incentive to live without his friend. While Thor would never have wished any misery on Balook, it still gratified him to be so strongly *needed.*

Then there was the time Thor himself had surgery for a small pollution-tumor on the lung. Air standards

The animal seemed to enjoy the programs too

were strict, but violations occurred, and there was considerable residual effect from the old days of uncontrolled waste. He was twelve then, and Balook was four. They had to let Balook visit *him*, for the animal was unmanageable otherwise. Balook no longer bawled, he bellowed. No stall would restrain his superelephantine bulk when he sulked. But the truth was that Thor himself did not prosper alone; that visit by the rhino was as necessary for his well-being as his had been for the rhino. He liked to think that Balook had understood that, and had raised his fuss for that reason.

Thor smiled, remembering how the tremendous humped nose had poked into the second storey window, horrifying an unwarned nurse. The special rhino smell had percolated through the building, generating consternation in the staff and delighted comments from the children, who were reminded of the zoo or circus. That first visit had done him much good—and so had the laugh. The other children at the hospital had been thrilled by the strange event, and thereafter Thor had been very popular with them. That, too, had been an unusual pleasure. Balook had made Thor a person of momentary distinction.

"What are you grinning about?" Scale demanded testily. "You don't seem to appreciate that this is a serious business, Nemmen! Five hundred million dollars on the line, and if he balks—"

Evidently they had made some plan, that Thor should have been paying attention to. "I wasn't laughing about what you said, sir," he admitted. "I just remembered how Balook scared that nurse when I was sick—"

"You weren't paying attention to what we said?" the man demanded ominously.

Thor made an embarrassed shrug. "I guess not."

"Listen, Nemmen, even a person of minimal intelligence—"

Skip interceded for him, as he often did. "The lad's honest, Don. Balook trusts him. That's what counts, isn't it? You know the farrier couldn't even trim his hooves if Thor wasn't there to tell Balook to lift his feet. So Thor thinks about Balook in off moments; that's what he's here for, not high finance. He's Balook's friend.''

Which was about as good a summary of Thor's place in the Project as could be offered. Skip had made Thor's inattention seem like an asset!

Scale sighed windily, blowing out his cheeks. It was a natural enough gesture, typical of him. Scale was always a bit grumpy. But this time it triggered an odd alarm in Thor.

For Scale's left hand came down to rest on the side table, on the trailing leads of the lie detector. And the needle shot over to FALSE. Thor's peripheral vision caught the motion; he had the sense not to look directly, but there was no question what it was. The needle normally rested on TRUE; motion could be only one way.

Scale was hiding something.

No—the man was merely tense because of Balook's breakout; naturally that tension registered on the detector. Thor cautioned himself about being too eager to blame the man he didn't like anyway.

''And that nurse incident *was* funny,'' Skip continued. ''Also the way Balook left droppings all over their ornamental lawn, with all the patients watching. Great fertilizer; we should've charged them for it! Can't think why the administrators weren't amused. Remember how that obnoxious hospital-ground bulldog went after him, and a pellet fell right on its head?''

Thor choked, and Scale finally had to smile. ''Served that canine right,'' he agreed. When it came to any threat against Balook, no matter how minor, Scale was one with Skip and Thor. "Lucky Balook didn't step on him." He removed his hand from the table, and the needle moved back to TRUE.

Sure, Scale was worried. But who was more worried about Balook's absence than himself, Thor wondered. He couldn't resist a comparison. Without looking, he put his own hand on the table, across the leads of the lie detector, as though by accident. His eyes flicked over to the meter.

The needle was holding steady about halfway toward FALSE.

Either Scale was twice as worried about Balook as Thor was—surely impossible!—or Scale had some guilty knowledge. It had to relate to Balook, for that was the subject of discussion.

Or, could it relate to Thor himself? Skip had just vouched for Thor's honesty, and Scale had sighed and touched the leads . . . and the needle had given him the lie. Did that make sense?

Skip turned to Thor. "As we see it, lad, you're our best hope. Balook will pay attention to you when he won't to us. He's too big to transport by truck; it would take a flatcar to carry him—"

"You can't put him in a box!" Thor cried. "Balook hates confinement. He's never—"

"That's what I'm saying, lad," Skip said gently. "Anything smaller than a barn makes him nervous, and his nervousness is like the rumble of a volcano. He has to come back under his own power, and nobody can lead him on a tether! He's stubborn as—"

"He's Balook's friend."

"As a rhino," Scale said. "And not one whit smarter."

"Sure he is!" Thor protested loyally.

Scale scowled. "Very well. One whit."

"So you'll have to ride him in," Skip concluded, overriding Thor's objection to Scale's comment.

"I ride him all the time! He guides perfectly!"

"Around the pasture, sure. But what about cross-country, watching out for people and traffic? It's a hostile world out there, lad—hostile for him and maybe for you too. If he spooked, you'd be finished."

"Balook would never hurt me!"

"Not intentionally," Skip said soberly.

"I'll bring him back!" Thor said. "Just as soon as I can find him!"

"He's naturally shy of people, and that's good," Skip said. "There's quite a bit of forest land around here, thanks to the ecology splurge of the Seventies. If he stays out of trouble a few more hours, maybe you can do it."

"But you'll have to run him down cross-country," Scale said. "A copter would spook him, even if we had one ready. So would a car, if it could get close."

"I know," Thor said eagerly. "I'll go on foot. I'm in pretty good condition, and he can't be far—"

"Lad, he walks at fifteen miles an hour, and runs at twenty-five or better," Skip said. "You'd never have a chance."

Again Thor had to convert to more familiar terms. Balook walked about twenty-four kilometers an hour, and ran at forty. Yes, that was fast, too fast for a man on foot to maintain, cross-country.

"Can you ride a bicycle?" Scale asked.

"Who can't?" Thor returned, surprised by the question. "I've got one at home. But how would I make it cross-country on wheels, let alone across streams and limited access routes?" Even as he spoke, he wondered why the man had brought it up. Scale could not be so far out of touch with reality as not to know that *everyone* rode bikes, and that Thor, like most others, had traveled thousands of kilometers, cumulative, in his life that way. It was excellent exercise for an isolated boy.

"I mean a high-tech bike," Scale said, frowning.

"Oh, sure, if I had one. Principle's the same."

"We've got a lightweight with boosters," Skip said.

"Been saving it for an emergency—and this is that. Think you could handle it?"

Thor's eyes went round. "That must be a thousand dollar machine!"

"Eight hundred and seventy-nine dollars, including booster fuel," Scale said. He knew the price of everything.

"Come on," Skip said. "We can't waste time."

The bike was beautiful. It had thin foam-metal tires and a twelve speed gearshift, and it weighed fifteen kilos. Two V-thrust boosters were mounted fore and aft, and there was a tube of energy syrup clamped to the frame.

"Remember," Skip warned. "The boosters are for emergency use only. They're warranted for fifteen minutes' air-time, and you can't count on more than a couple minutes beyond that. Don't waste them!"

Thor nodded, licking his lips. What a machine! He had had dreams of riding a bike like this, but the reality was hard to assimilate so suddenly. In fact, it seemed too convenient, having this fabulous machine here. If Scale knew something, something that Thor might find out, and if he had known the appeal that such a bike would have for any boy—could the bike be somehow booby-trapped?

No, he was veering into paranoia! He did not much like Scale, and the feeling was mutual, but Scale was not out to get rid of him, because Scale knew Thor was good for Balook. The bicycle made sense. Only a copter could locate Balook rapidly, and the two-day delay for requisitioning made that pointless. Naturally they wanted little publicity, for that would alert the curiosity seekers. Balook was a tremendous curiosity!

Skip had known about the bike too. So it hadn't just been brought in for this occasion. Skip would never betray anyone. So the safest assumption was that the bike was legitimate, and that Scale's guilt, as shown by the FALSE reading, was about something else.

Was Scale himself in some way responsible for Balook's breakout? That seemed crazy, yet it could account for his secret reaction. Scale's whole effort to recover Balook would be a lie, if he *wanted* the animal loose, perhaps even dead. But he would have to *seem* to do everything to save Balook.

Thor shook his head. It was all too complicated, right now. Scale was an honest man, and devoted to Balook's interests; he had proved that long ago. In fact his job depended on Balook. Maybe the lie detector had somehow miscued.

Probably Don Scale would put out a private police alert. But the police could not bring Balook back alive. Only Thor himself could do that—and he had to approach the huge rhino alone.

"Get moving, lad," Skip said.

Thor mounted the bike. It was a little large for him. Skip lowered the seat and handlebars and made other adjustments, quickly. "Here," he said. "You'll need a credit key. Take mine."

"Thanks," Thor said, gratified at the man's trust. "But it'll only be a couple hours—"

"Maybe. But we'd better play it safe. Here's a phone—you know how to operate it?"

Thor glanced at the instrument—and did a double-take. It was a ring-transceiver, the kind that buzzed or glowed to signal an incoming call, and had a button setting for two-way dialogue. It could call out only to the preset station, but was otherwise a competent phone.

Awed, he slipped it on his ring finger, but found it too large. He tried the middle finger, and that was better. "Yes, I can use it."

"We'll notify your folks," Skip said. "In case you don't catch him soon. Just keep going, and keep us posted." Then Skip gave the bike a starting push, and Thor was on his way.

THE BICYCLE WAS so smooth-riding that at first Thor thought something was wrong. He was used to a middleweight machine, twice as heavy as this, with inflated composition tires. The foam metal on this one flexed away from ground irregularities, providing a special spring that made bumps a pleasure. The guidance was so light as to seem automatic; he could steer entirely by shifts of his body weight, even on rough ground, so that his hands were free for other tasks. That was a trick his regular bike could not do, not cross-country; he had the memory of old bruises to prove it. The gears were pressure coordinated, so that changing pedal force adjusted the ratio for maximum efficiency; he could turn it off when his definitions differed from those of the machine. The brake was American style, with optional hand brakes; he could have it either way.

Thor was in love with the bike before he had covered

the first five hundred meters. It was a boy's dream machine.

He was at the break in the fence so quickly he was surprised. Now he could test the first special feature. He approached the gap broadside and touched the booster switch. The hot gas fired out instantly, down and back and to the sides, lifting the bike high while maintaining its balance. Too high—he was heading for the unbroken top strand!

He cut the boosters. They diminished slowly, not dousing entirely, so that he first leveled off, then slowly descended. He passed safely under the wire and glided to the ground beyond. He was elated; the boosters had worked perfectly, being fail-safe and foolproof. But he knew he would have to be more careful in the future; he could have caught his neck on the wire and been knocked right off the bike, six meters in the air. He could have broken something, and had a nasty electrical shock in the bargain. Those wires were paired; it was not necessary to make contact with the ground to receive the current. Birds stayed clear.

Had Scale been hoping for some such miscue? No, Thor couldn't believe that! Scale was concealing something, but he was no murderer. In fact, Thor knew that Scale no longer wanted to be rid of Thor, because of Thor's value to the project. So the mystery remained: why had the lie detector given him the lie?

Now it was time to be alert for Balook's traces. They were clear enough: broken branches, huge footprints in the soft ground, and occasional swatches of shed hair. It was no longer the fine, soft fur of calfhood; today Balook's hair was sparse and bristly, more like pine needles than fur. In fact, the huge animal used the spokelike hairs of his legs to sense obstructions; it wasn't always convenient to look. This was surely one reason he was able to move and forage well at night; his legs took care of themselves.

There was no visible damage to the upper foliage. The fallen branches were from the lower branches, torn off by the animal's massive torso. Balook was traveling, not browsing, and that was ominous. Usually he could not resist high, fresh leaves and twigs. He had to consume tremendous amounts each day, to maintain his vigor. That was why he required a formidable forest pasture; the trees of a small one would soon be denuded.

Was Balook sick? That could account for erratic behavior and the loss of appetite. There could be some special malady; there were volumes they had yet to learn about *Baluchitherium*. But Thor had always been the first person Balook turned to in time of distress. Also, this direct route away from the ranch was not that of a confused, ill animal. There was purpose in it.

Balook was going somewhere. His trail was neither meandering in the fashion of exploration nor arrow-straight in the fashion of a stampede. The wide spacing of the giant three-toed prints showed he was traveling at cruising velocity: about forty kilometers per hour. As fast as Thor could ride this bike across this terrain! But of course the animal would not keep it up; Balook was really not a running creature, and soon overheated when he put out too much energy. He had ways of handling that, but seldom drew on them.

Yet obviously Balook had already traveled faster and

farther than normal, and the trail showed no sign of easing. This was something new to their experience, this motivation to travel. Balook was the only creature of his kind man had ever seen alive. He had put on a lot of muscle recently, especially in the legs and chest—more than he seemed to require for the normal routine. Maybe this was an aspect of his maturity. Maybe now he could sustain a rapid pace. The physical situation was less perplexing than the rationale: *why* was Balook doing it?

The barricades of the freak zoo loomed ahead. Of course that wasn't its real name, and it wasn't a zoo at all. It was part of the Project, though it lay beyond the pasture. There had been abortive experiments on animal tissue, preparing the way for the final success that was Balook. This was the original laboratory.

Balook was a strange creature, in more senses than one or two, and the freak zoo helped show why. Computer technology had merged with genetics to make it possible. Theoretically any animal, real or imaginary, could be formed. But there had been surprises, for the genetic code was complex beyond man's imagination. Some of the failures had been gut-wrenchingly grotesque, and even the successes, such as Balook, had had astonishing aspects.

One of the more significant surprises had been the way Balook handled heat. In cold weather he had little trouble, as he achieved his grown mass; he simply exercised, and his body and hide hoarded the heat. But in hot weather, when he overexerted himself, he had more of a problem, for he did not sweat. He tended to forage at night, when the heat generated by his motion compensated for the cool of the evening. But he could handle day too. He kept his body mostly in the shade of the trees, avoiding the direct sun. But even so, he grew hot—and it turned out that this was part of his makeup. When he was conserving heat, his outer body cooled, much as did the hands of a man, but more extensively; snow could actually fall on his back without melting rapidly. He had a blubbery layer of fat that could cool almost to freezing without damage. In summer this same layer could heat to well above the danger point for man, so that the hide felt burningly hot, and radiated heat efficiently. Balook could also conserve that excess heat, as night approached, and use it as a buffer against the developing cold. It was a sophisticated mechanism for survival—all hidden there in the small print of the genetic code, not understood until it manifested in life.

How was it that Balook's kind had become extinct, when it was so much better equipped to survive than the cousin rhinos that did carry on to the present day? That was one of the mysteries that remained unresolved.

But Thor had a more immediate concern. Could Balook have come to meet his soul-cousins in the zoo? No, his trail skirted the barricades, and nothing was broken. Thor heard a grunting inside that was probably the six-legged pig. Once it had been thought that creatures like this would prove the gene-splicing technique, but opponents had claimed that fetal surgery accounted for the extra legs. Indeed, it could have, for that aspect of medicine had progressed too. So the pig, an actual success, was a practical failure; it was too easy to disbelieve.

The majority of the experiments had been true failures, even those that lived. It was illegal to kill any wildlife, so these had to be maintained for their full natural spans. Rather, their unnatural spans. Thor had never been inside the compound, and could only speculate what other monsters were hidden from public view, the shame of science.

Thor rode on, glad that Balook had passed by the zoo. Balook was no freak! The proof of the technique could not be in the recreation of an existing animal, for there would always be the suspicion that a natural embryo had been substituted for the laboratory specimen. Indeed, the process started with natural tissue, whose genetic blueprint was then modified by radiation and laser surgery and chemistry.

Thus the decision had settled on the past: the recreation of some long-extinct animal, perfect in every detail. No slight-of-hand could explain *that* away, or make it smell of freak or fluke. To make it impressive, for that inevitable day the Project would face appropriations cutbacks, they chose a large animal. Not a dinosaur; the reptilian environment would have been too difficult to duplicate on that scale. Not a sea creature, for that would not have been suitably visible.

So it was *Baluchitherium*, the hornless rhinoceros of the Miocene Epoch, thirteen to twenty million years ago. The experts had used a battery of computers to analyze the rhinoceros chromosomes, then had done the laser surgery on the living tissue: the fertilized rhino egg. A few small changes, meticulously scripted to

So the pig, an actual success, was a practical failure

make it conform to the pattern derived from painstakingly analyzed *Baluchitherium* bones, and the sample was ready.

It died. They made adjustments. There had been a series of seemingly minor options, choices between settings that seemed to make no difference. Evidently this was not the case. They made changes, and tried again.

That one also died. So did the next. And the following efforts, as they changed the pattern desperately, seeking the key to survival. They added larger sections of what had been assumed to be counterproductive elements, and tinkered with those. More deaths. But the failures were showing signs of progress, hanging on longer before expiring.

A hundred or more expensive cultures failed—but in the end five of them formed embryos, of which three developed imperfectly. What distinguished the survivors from the non-survivors was unclear. One of the successes was dispatched to another laboratory for study. The other became, at last, Balook.

Thor had named him, actually. The nine year old boy had found the full proper name too cumbersome. *Baluchitherium*, derived from the place where the first fossil bones of the original creatures had been found: Baluchistan, Asia. Present-day Pakistan and Iran. A related type was called *Indricotherium*; there was some question which was the most accurate designation for this re-created creature. But now everyone used Thor's nickname, and Balook answered to it, at least when Thor called. Ba-look, with the accent on the second syllable, to rhyme with "spook." Ba-LOOK-i-THER-ium. Few folk had ever heard of this creature, the largest mammal ever to walk the earth. One day that ignorance would change.

Now Balook was seven years old, dating from the time he should normally have been born. Of course he had never been born; he had just grown from test-tube culture to incubator item to laboratory specimen to stable. He was not yet mature; he would fill out slowly for several more years.

Just as Thor himself would, he reflected as he pedaled along the haphazard trail. It wasn't bad traveling, so far, because the forest land in the vicinity of the ranch was kept clear of underbrush, and Balook naturally chose the firmest footing. One misstep could kill an animal that size, because the height and mass of the body were both so great. Balook took care never to misstep.

The tractor-trails passed through at regular intervals, for the trees were constantly thinned, trimmed, watered and fertilized. Balook's spoor was following one of those trails at present.

Suddenly Thor was facing a moving tractor. The machine was just heaving over the rise that had hidden it, and the hum of the electric motor was scarcely audible even at close range. It was robot controlled, of course, and not programmed to stop for intruders.

The machine came on so swiftly that Thor had to career off the path to get out of the way. The solid machine moved on past, dragging a parcel of trimmings behind it, taking no notice of him.

Suppose Balook ran into such a tractor?

Thor smiled. That was no problem. Balook would either avoid the thing or step over it. Balook distrusted machinery, perhaps because it vaguely resembled an animal but had no proper smell or manner.

Now he came to a stream. Balook had crossed and gone on. Thor knew he should dismount and carry his bike across, but he couldn't resist using the boosters again. He touched the switch, moving it only slightly so that he did not get too much lift. Even so, he caught a glimpse of distant power line towers, like skeletal giants marching across the horizon. What would the world do without power! He sailed across the rocky water and landed neatly on the other side. Actually, this maneuver saved time, and used only a few seconds of boost; he hadn't really wasted it.

Why had Balook broken out? It didn't make sense!

Suppose someone had intruded, and fired at Balook? Skip had pooh-poohed the notion of someone shooting at the huge animal. But Skip knew it had happened before.

Private guns were outlawed, true—but the law was violated widely, and only enforced when someone got hurt. Unauthorized people did not carry guns openly, but could have concealed weapons. Many outsiders resented the resources used in the Project. They felt that the development of an extinct animal was wasted effort, since the world was already pinched and overcrowded. Some of those same people, oddly, also objected to the "waste" of unoccupied national forests. It seemed that they had a low tolerance for any land or any thing that did not contribute directly to their comfort, and they took no comfort in nature. That might have accounted for the old-timer who had one morning fired a .22 bullet into Balook's shoulder.

The man had been arrested and fined, and of course his gun had been confiscated. Balook recovered; he was too massive to be seriously hurt by that caliber. But he still carried the tiny scar, and remembered the pain. He was afraid of the sound of gunfire, or any similar noise. Once workmen had used a power riveter for an addition to the stable, and Balook had gone wild. He had knocked down the stable walls faster than the workmen were putting them up. So if anyone had come near the fence this time and made a loud noise, even firing blanks . . .

Could Don Scale have set off a firecracker behind Balook, making him leap through the barrier? No, no, the suspicion was paranoid! Scale simply would not do that, ever. Even if someone else had done it, this would not explain why Balook had kept on going. He might have crashed out and run for a distance, yes, but not this purposeful journey west.

Thor was breathing hard, now, though he was an experienced biker. The terrain was becoming rougher as the trail neared the edge of the cleared forest. There was a road a kilometer or so ahead; Thor was familiar with this section. Why would Balook head for a highway?

Balook did not know the motor-vehicle road was there, of course. Maybe he had stopped when he saw it, and Thor would find him waiting, bewildered. Mission accomplished?

Thor condemned the destructive ignorance of the pot-shotter, but he knew that the evil was more than one man or one gun, and could not be eliminated by one arrest. Even now there was a legislative narrowness that condemned the Project as an inflationary waste. Skip had spoken of this attitude often, spitting deliberately on the ground as if there were a bad taste in his mouth. Indeed, Balook had cost a lot of money. Don Scale had mentioned five hundred million dollars, but Thor was sure that was only a small part of it.

The truth was that Balook was significant, not only as a living unextinct animal and the largest land mammal who ever lived, but as the key to the creation of new forms of life. All the failed experiments, the mutated animal fetuses—these had led up to the first real success. Balook had shown the way, so that it could be done for other creatures or even human beings without the same horrible mistakes. This would surely benefit man and save many times its cost of development, in the long run. Skip had discussed this, too, and Thor had pretty well assimilated the entire dialogue. This was one type of study at which this poor student had had real motivation to succeed.

But he did not need intellectual reasons to help Balook! He loved the big animal, and that would have sufficed even if nothing else mattered.

Balook's trail intersected a bicycle route, which was not surprising, as these trails crisscrossed the nation as well as the region. The prints followed this. Excellent; Thor could make real time along this stretch. He was lucky he lived in a time when self-propelled vehicles—*human*, not motor propelled—were the main form of private transportation. Even ten years ago there had been more cars than bikes!

He cocked his head, hearing a noise: a kind of thud-thud-thud! Could that be Balook? It was off the trail, but the rhino could have circled back, losing the way. It really didn't sound like Balook; still . . .

Thor left the path and pedaled across, orienting on the noise. The closer he got, the less familiar it sounded. There was something sinister about it. What could Balook be doing?

Then he broke upon the source—and was shocked. It wasn't Balook. It was a tree poacher.

The man was pounding in the last of four anchor-stakes, using a muffled sledge to stifle the noise. The tree was already guyed by three slow-stretch springs, the kind that would let it down no faster than a meter in five or six seconds, if the anchors were secure. A silent felling, and a careful coverup—so that after the theft there would be nothing but uninterrupted forest floor. With luck, the crime would not have been discovered until the next tree inventory survey.

Except for the coincidence of Thor's search for Balook.

Fury blinded him. "Stop, thief!" Thor cried—and realized instantly that he was being melodramatic and foolish. For this was no petty unpremeditated violation like casual mayhem; this was wilderness despoilation.

The poacher whirled around, raising his sledge. Thor knew he was in trouble. The poacher would be reconditioned if caught, and was ready to kill to avoid that fate. To many people, death was hardly worse than reconditioning; both processes destroyed a person's present individuality.

Thor's hand jumped to the booster control. He shot upward as the slow sledge swung. It caught his rear wheel, glancingly, knocking him out of control. He hadn't cleared in time!

But the very distortion of his travel helped him, for as the bike wobbled in the air, the booster jets intersected the body of the man below. They were strong and hot at this close range, as they had to be to maintain the weight of bike and rider. They pushed the man back, burning him. He cursed, scrambling clear.

Now Thor remembered the phone. He pushed down its button. "There's a poacher here!" he gasped to Skip.

"Oh there is, is there!" Skip answered grimly. "Okay, lad—we've got a fix on it. We'll catch him. You go on about your business."

Thor returned to Balook's trail, shaken by the episode. He had just sent a living man into reconditioning! The police would be landing within a minute. No copters were convenient for a five hundred million dollar

Baluchitherium search, but poachers at a fixed location were another matter. No chance for the man to flee undetected.

The poachers were getting bolder, to operate right here in protected forest land! He had known they existed; the newscasts mentioned such outrages frequently. But to actually encounter such a criminal in the flesh—that left his heart pounding unpleasantly.

He knew why they did it. Fresh wood brought a phenomenal price on the black market. Still . . .

Sometimes Thor wished he had been born sooner, so that he could have seen the incredible squandering of resources that continued even after everyone knew to what disaster it was leading. Maybe he could have done something about it. Certainly *he* would never have been so stupid as to use pure water to flush high-grade sewage into the sea, thus destroying all three elements: water, recoverable wastes, and ocean environment. Today water was for drinking, sewage for fertilizer, and the sea for fish. Today was civilized. Once he had visited a sea-floor farm and seen the swimming crops, and touched the tentacle of a tame octopus. The huge squid were penned separately, as they could never be trusted, but the octopi could be handled.

Still, there was room for improvement, and Balook was showing the way. Other worlds could be explored, worlds hostile to man, because the techniques that had fashioned Balook could in due course remake man himself. A strain of human being adapted to cold and low oxygen could colonize Mars; another strain adapted to heat and darkness could settle on Venus, if a way were found to handle the enormous atmospheric pressure there.

But Balook would help most right here on Earth. Meat was scarce and expensive now, but wonderful meat-producing strains could be developed, not in decades or even in years, but in months—once the bio-computers tackled the problem. People could be fed at a fraction of the present cost per food-pound. Why not a bacon bush or a steak tree, when it came down to it? Or a steak-snake; that sounded better.

A mosquito stung him on the arm. Thor slapped at it. One thing about the pesticide moratorium: the pests survived. Theoretically biological warfare against the insects kept them under control, but nature was always a jump or two ahead. However, the Balook technique could produce special insectivores, bug eaters supreme.

He smiled. Bug-eyed monsters—with an eye for bugs.

Then he realized that his flight of fancy was unrealistic. Insects and arachnids had their place too; they were needed for fertilization of many plants, and as food for birds. He had been too narrow. Perhaps it would be better to develop a kind of human being whose blood made mosquitoes sick. That made him smile; he had a mental picture of a mosquito turning green in the snoot and buzzing anxiously for a basin.

Maybe there could even be life forms that fed on contaminating radiation, improving the environment further. The prospects seemed endless. But all the local folk seemed to worry about was Balook's size and the "waste" of funds.

Thor shook his head—and realized that he had just

lost Balook's trail. He had been blithely zooming along the bikeway, and had missed the place where Balook turned off. Damn!

He slowed and turned about, furious with himself. He would have to stop thinking to himself so much. That was a bad habit he had gotten into in the course of his years of semi-isolation from people his own age. If Balook got in trouble in the extra time made by this needless delay—

The radio buzzed. Thor jumped guiltily. He turned it on. "Right here," he said.

"Skip, again. We got the poacher. Mean customer! This will clear up a number of unsolved thefts in this neighborhood. Congratulations!"

"That's great!" Thor said, relieved that Skip hadn't found out about his losing the trail. But how could Skip have learned? It was a pointless concern.

"Now about Balook. You're way off—"

Thor gulped audibly.

"No fault of yours, lad," Skip continued. "He's been sighted thirty-five miles west of the ranch. That's about a two hour start on you, at your rate through the rough. Not as bad as I figured, but bad enough. Can you catch him?"

Thor spied Balook's trail again, going west, into high brush. Balook was tall enough to step over most of the bushes without flattening them. That meant an almost impenetrable wall of foliage barred Thor's way. No wonder he had missed it!

"Not a chance," Thor said. "I'll have to carry the bike through this mess, or boost over. Unless I go around. But that would add a lot of mileage."

"Don't waste your boost!" Skip said, alarmed. "Look, lad—that was a chance sighting. A housewife who thought she was dreaming, but called the police anyway, just in case. They told her the perspective must have made a stray horse seem bigger than it was. Not many outsiders know much about Balook, you know."

Thor hadn't known. He had assumed that his knowledge was common, and that the criticism of the Project relayed to him was from the general public. He should have known better. He had become insular, locked mainly in the world he shared with Balook. Yet a news blackout could have suppressed even such episodes as the hospital visit, so that only vague rumors circulated. But he hardly cared to discuss that now. "What happened?"

"They called us. They've been alerted, and warned to stay clear, but you know how snoopy folk get. They aren't going to stay clear long, especially if anybody gets hurt. You've got to get over there now. We're sending a car around to give you a lift."

"But a car will spook Balook!"

"Not if it lets you off a mile or two from him. We've got to take that chance, lad! Now you put your signal on and scoot over to the nearest motor vehicle lane, and the car will find you in a few minutes."

"Okay," Thor said, slightly disturbed at this change in plans. Was Skip subtly letting him know that there was a lack of confidence in his abilities? He found the "Signal" setting on the ring radio and left it on. There was no audible response; there wasn't supposed to be.

He turned his bike about again and pedaled north. Actually he'd be glad for a rest; he wasn't used to this strenuous and extended effort. A cross-country pursuit was different from a few kilometers on an established bikeway.

The car was prompt. It rolled up as he intersected the motor lane. It was an automatic electric: no driver.

He folded the bike and set it in the rear rack, then climbed into the car. The motor whined smoothly as the vehicle accelerated down the lane, achieving a speed no human driver would have trusted.

Thor hardly had a chance to relax, before the car slowed. Sixty kilometers—in twenty minutes!

He got out and unfolded the bicycle. The car moved smoothly away. Balook's trail was visible where it crossed the lane. Good enough.

The land was more open here, and Thor was not familiar with it. It was not easy pedaling, for there were rocks and holes in the ground; a semi-wilderness park. Balook's trail was harder to follow, because there were fewer trees to show damage and the hard terrain hardly showed his imprint. Also, the path was no longer straight, for Balook was now traveling from tree to tree. Not to eat; he was seeking partial shade and concealment, for he liked neither the sunlight nor the open range.

Again Thor marveled at Balook's imperative. For a primarily nocturnal, forest-shade creature to charge out into unshaded territory by day, with the problem of heat dissipation that brought, and keep going—he had to have some truly compelling reason. But what could it be?

The animal had to be close, for this was where he had been sighted. Within a couple of kilometers. How

Sixty kilometers in twenty minutes!

far could he have strayed in twenty minutes?

Confidently Thor went on, traversing the difficult landscape. He felt much refreshed by the brief rest, and by the knowledge that he was now close. The foam metal wheels absorbed much of the constant jarring, and the shock absorbers helped too, but the pedaling was still stiff. At any moment, now, he would spy Balook's hulking body . . .

Yet several kilometers passed, with no more direct sign of the quarry. Finally Thor touched his ring. "Skip, are you sure he's here?" he asked when the man answered. "I can't find him."

"No, I'm *not* sure," Skip replied worriedly. "We don't know how long it took the woman to report, and there may have been delay in relaying the message. Don't forget Balook's moving right along, too."

"He's slowed down," Thor said. "He passed this section in sunlight, so it can't have been too long ago."

"How do you know that?"

Thor explained about the tree-to-tree pattern of the trail. Skip whistled. "You're a regular Sherlock Holmes, lad! Smart thinking. But the sun's well up now; he could still be an hour ahead of you, which means several hours to catch up. Sorry, lad; I misjudged it."

Thor sighed. That action reminded him of Scale's sigh, and the movement of the lie detector's needle. Had something happened to Balook, and this was a false trail, complete with false sightings? Ridiculous, yet . . . "Well, at least I'm sixty kilos closer than I was."

"I wonder where he's going?" Skip mused.

"If we knew that, I wouldn't have to chase him!" Thor snapped. The idea of Balook going without him still hurt—if Balook *had* gone of his own accord. Yet who could have forced the animal?

"Sure, lad." Skip paused. "Okay: suppose we give you another lift, since that's the way he's going."

Thor's legs were tiring again from the rough pedaling. "Might as well," he agreed, as if it were an incidental decision.

The car took him west ten kilometers, and he found the trail. Then it took him twenty more, and he lost the trail. He had to backtrack, cursing. The reason became plain: Balook had changed course. He was now bearing northwest. So Thor hopped in that direction—and lost the trail again.

Balook was wandering, going now north and now south, but averaging west. He still wasn't eating. The oddity of this travel was increasing.

Then another eyewitness report came in, and the car took Thor to that spot. This sighting was recent; Thor knew he was only fifteen minutes behind Balook now. It was late in the day, two hundred fifty kilometers west of the Project grounds. Balook had to be tired, hungry, and hot; now was the time to catch him!

Thor pedaled furiously, aided by another bike path parallel to the trail. There was a large river a few kilos north, so he knew Balook would not drift far that way. The animal had never been exposed to deep water.

This time he was in luck. He heard the thud of great hooves ahead, for Balook shook the ground when he walked swiftly. Thor doubled his effort, heedless of the pain in his thighs and calves, racing along the path.

The noise of Balook's progress grew louder. But it was hard to gain on him, because the beast's pace was almost as swift as the bike's. Thor raced a good two kilometers without actually catching sight of his quarry.

Things could have been worse, he thought breathlessly. Now there was a lot of parkland and cultured wilderness, thanks to the current land administration policies. So Balook had been able to survive, so far. But sooner or later the huge rhino would blunder into a major highway or residential development, and then it would be disaster.

Thor topped a small rise and came into the clear section beside the river. The pretty water spread ahead. And there, at the edge, just rising from a drink, stood Balook.

He was like a heavyset, powerful, huge-footed horse—twice the height of any equine that ever lived. His massive shoulders towered over five meters above the ground. His head, a meter and a half long, looked tiny compared to the huge body and massive neck. The great humped nose was lifting to sniff the air, and the fleshy, almost prehensile upper lip was extended to help. The little ears were cocked, listening.

The rays of the declining sun reflected off the surface of the water and silhouetted the magnificent figure, making the brown hide glow. Balook was no ugly duckling now. He was the largest and most beautiful creature ever to walk the earth!

"Balook!" Thor cried gladly. He really was crying, for there were tears on his cheeks, tears of admiration and relief. He had found Balook, and Balook was all right. They were together again!

And there at the edge stood Balook

Balook heard him. The high head swung around, the thick skin of the neck creasing. The little tail swished, in that way it had. The tails of horses were formidable fly-swatters, always in motion in summer, but Balook's hide was too tough for most flies, and at this time of day too hot for them too. Thus the tail was used more for expression than for business, though it could strike hard if motivated.

The animal took a step toward Thor, then halted, lip quivering, nose elevated. Then Balook turned and plunged into the river.

Amazed, Thor pulled up and watched. "But you can't swim!" he protested. But he quickly saw that this was irrelevant. Balook splashed across, his legs so long that the water never touched his belly. Was he trying to use it to cool himself? No, for then he should have ducked down into it. The river was a good twenty meters across, but soon Balook was stepping into the forest on the other side.

Thor stood gaping. Why had Balook run? He had heard and recognized Thor!

Angrily Thor touched the booster setting. The jets fired and the bike rose—almost straight up. He had forgotten that he had no forward motion, no inertia to carry him across. The slant of the jets was set to maintain forward progress, not to initiate it. Quickly he adjusted the tilt of the jets.

The bike looped about in the air and flung him off, five meters over the river.

Thor hit the water on his back with a monstrous splash. He sank, but fortunately he had landed in deep-enough water. In a moment he stroked to the surface, gasping, his nose stinging with sucked-in fluid. His back was smarting, but he wasn't really hurt.

The bike was bobbing along in the gentle current, its hollow tubing causing it to float. Thor swam over and recovered it, then sidestroked for shore, hauling it along. He found his footing, stood, and waded out.

The machine was intact, since the same blind luck that had saved Thor's neck had plunged the bike into the water instead of the hard ground. The booster jets had been extinguished; there was no way to tell how much boost had been wasted before the fuel cut off. There would have to be several hours of drying before the jets worked, and then they might be unreliable. Still, it was a better outcome than he felt he really deserved.

Bedraggled, dripping, and suddenly cold, Thor gazed across the water. He could never catch Balook now. He would have to resume the chase tomorrow. But that was not what bothered him most.

He was Balook's friend, his only real friend, the one person the huge animal really trusted. Always before, Balook had come running at his call, eager for companionship and the interactions of the day. No power on earth should have been able to sever that years-long bond of friendship and need. Not while they both lived.

Yet Balook had seen and recognized Thor—and fled.

"I THINK YOU had better give up the chase, lad," Skip said. "You're lucky you didn't kill yourself—"

"No!" Thor cried. "I know I can catch him, now!"

"But if, as you say, he's deliberately avoiding you—"

Thor shook his head, more in dismay than negation. That still hurt, even after his troubled night's sleep at the hostel. "I just have to go after him, that's all."

Skip's sigh carried through the ring radio. "That's what I told Don."

Thor sat up straight, alarmed. "You've been talking to Mr. Scale?"

Now Skip laughed in that easy way of his. "Sure, lad. He's my boss, you know."

"Is he there now?"

"No, he's out seeing about the break in the fence. Why?"

Thor's hands were suddenly clammy. "He—I didn't want to say this, but—"

"Sounds like something you'd better have out, lad!"

"I guess. He—you know that lie detector? The one he uses to—"

"I know it."

"His hand touched it, when we were in the office, and—and the needle went straight to FALSE. I—"

"I saw it too, lad."

"I don't know what he—" Thor paused, doing a doubletake. "You saw it too?"

"Listen, lad, Don Scale's an honest man. He wouldn't hurt Balook. If he's hiding something, and I would guess he is, it's because he's been ordered to hide it. Don't go getting any ideas about him letting Balook out; he cares for the rhino the same way you do, only he doesn't show it. So he covers up with talk of money and such. He's with us—you believe that."

"I know that, I guess. But—"

"But you keep your mouth shut about that meter reading. Maybe Don *does* know something about what happened to Balook. But we've got to work with him and trust him. *I* trust him, and I know that when the truth's out, he'll be all right. Now you just go on after Balook, and maybe we'll find out the whole story."

"Okay, Skip," Thor said dubiously. But the knowledge that his friend had also seen the movement of the needle on the lie detector encouraged him; Skip was better equipped to know what to believe.

"We'll keep the car handy, in case he's moving during the night again."

"He's got to sleep sometime!" But they really did not know how long the huge animal could keep going, when he wanted to. Ordinarily, night would be Balook's preferred time for traveling.

They played leapfrog again, all day, and still didn't catch up. Balook was moving rapidly ahead, into a mild west wind. Thor's muscles were sore despite the help of the car.

What was wrong with the animal? It was as though Balook was running faster, now that he knew Thor was on his trail. The rhino had traveled almost two hundred kilometers this day, through field and forest, across highways and rivers, going—where?

And what was Scale's secret? If Skip said it was okay, then it was okay, but it remained as mysterious as Balook's flight. If Scale knew something . . .

But his questions had no answers. As Skip said: he would just have to find Balook and get his answer.

On the third morning that answer abruptly materialized. Balook's tracks went up to a large fenced yard and through a gaping hole. It would have been easy for the animal to circle around the fence and go on, for this farm was in a pleasantly forested region. But Balook had broken in.

There was something here he wanted. But *what*?

Thor walked his bicycle through the gap, following the trail. But soon he lost it; there were too many tracks pointing in too many directions. What had Balook been *doing* here? Trampling down the whole farm?

Then he heard it: the sound of branches breaking as a huge animal browsed. Balook was eating again!

At last he caught up. "Balook!" he cried.

The animal turned, the folds of skin changing. The great head came into view.

Thor stared. *It* wasn't Balook!

But it *was Baluchitherium.* A different one, smaller, under five meters tall at the shoulders, and less heavily muscled. But definitely the same breed.

Which was impossible. Balook was the only one of his kind.

Suddenly the image of the lie detector returned, the needle reading FALSE. Balook—unique? Don Scale must have known there was another one!

"Well, hello!"

Thor looked toward the voice, startled. It was a girl of about his own age, rather pretty, with flouncing brown curls and eyes to match.

"You're a bit off the bikeway," she said. "This is private property."

"I was looking for Balook," Thor said, out of sorts.

"This is a *Baluchitherium,*" she said, gesturing to the animal. "But you can't have her, you know."

Her? A female *Baluchitherium*! "So that's it!" Thor cried. "He must have smelled her from all that distance, when the wind was right!"

The girl approached the animal, putting her arm across the tremendous nose that descended to meet her. "I take it you're associated with the one that broke in here this morning?"

"I am. Where is he?"

But no reply was necessary. Now Balook's head rose beyond the female.

"Satisfied?" the girl asked.

"I came a long way to find him!" Thor said defensively.

"I'll bet," she agreed. "We didn't know there *was*

It was a girl of about his own age, rather pretty . . .

another *Baluchitherium.* Mine's called Theria."

"Mine's Balook. I'm Thor. Thor Nemmen."

"I'm Barbara Hartford. Call me Barb. C'mon, you'd better come inside and clean up. You're a mess."

"But Balook—"

"He's not interested in you. He's not going anywhere."

"He's my fricnd!" Thor said hotly.

"Very well. Call him."

Thor called. "Balook!" But Balook paid him no attention.

"See?" Barb said. "Theria's the same way, now. Yesterday she was eager for my call, today she's got other concerns. She only noses me in passing. Why didn't you keep your animal penned?"

"How?" Thor asked sourly.

"I was being facetious. Come on."

Thor came. There really wasn't much else to do, and he was grimy from the morning's chase.

There followed a rush of introductions, as he met the personnel of Theria's domain. It was very like Balook's. Now he knew: this was where the second successful embryo had been taken. It had not been destroyed in laboratory experimentation, as he had supposed; it had been saved, and raised with the same care as Balook.

But why? And why hadn't anyone been told? So much trouble and anguish could have been spared!

"C'mon, let's walk," Barb said abruptly. Thor complied, uncertain what else there was to do. He didn't like this situation, the strangeness of two *Baluchither-*

iums, the hurt of being ignored by his friend, of being lied to by—someone.

She guided him out across the field and pasture and into the healthy forest of beech and oak, the intermediate foliage of the big trees pruned well back. Balook liked beechnuts and acorns; evidently Theria did too. They came to a grassy glade surrounded by young fir trees, where the sunlight slanted down in the center.

Barb flopped on the warm grass. She was a tomboy, lanky in her jeans and plaid shirt. Her brown curls fell across her face, half hiding it as she peered up at him.

Thor stood beside her, awkwardly. "C'mon," she said. "Join the crowd. Sit down."

"Okay." He sat down.

"You aren't much for conversation, are you!" she exclaimed.

"You wanted to talk, not me."

She rolled over on her back, looking at the sky. "I figured you'd have something to say."

"Damn it, what's there to say!" Thor cried angrily.

She smiled. "Now *that's* more like it! Why are you mad?"

"I chased all this way after Balook, and now he—" Thor broke off, exasperated. "Why did I bother?"

" 'Cause you love him," she said.

"I didn't say that!" But he realized he should have said it. Now he was stuck on the wrong foot.

"Why, then?"

"Oh, forget it!"

"I think it's sort of great," she said. "The two of them have been alone, all these years, and now they're together."

"Balook wasn't alone!"

"You know what I mean. Every creature needs its own kind. You wouldn't want to spend the rest of your life with only Balook for company, would you?"

"Yes I would!"

She rolled over again. "You're hung up, know that?"

"Yeah? What are you doing with Theria, then? Don't you *care*?"

"Sure I care! I love her. I love her more'n anything, and I'm not ashamed to say it. But I want *her* to be happy, too."

"Well, I want Balook happy!"

"He's happy now," she said.

Thor shook his head. "Oh, damn, what's the use!"

"You sure are great at swearing! Know any other words?"

"No!" Thor snapped, flushing. How could he have gotten so firmly on the wrong foot, without even trying?

They were silent for a while.

"Oh, c'mon," she said at last. "We're in this together. We should get to know each other. *That's* why I asked you here, you know."

Thor had cooled off, and was sorry for his gruffness. "I guess so."

"I mean, we're probably the only two people who ever existed as official companions for *Baluchitheria*. There weren't any people around in the Miocene period."

"Epoch."

"What? Oh—Miocene. Epoch. Yes, if you want to be technical."

"No, I don't care. It was a long time ago."

She changed the subject. "How did it start, with you?"

"I was just a nosy kid, poking about. I found Balook, and he was lonely."

"Like you."

"Yes, like me!" he snapped. "What's it to you?"

"I was lonely too," she said. "Still am."

"Oh." He considered for a moment, his emotions fuzzed. "Well, they tried to break it up, and Balook wouldn't let them. I was the only one he cared for. Then."

"Theria was having trouble too. I guess when they saw how it was with you—how good you were for Balook—they knew what to do. So they looked for someone for Theria, here, and they set it up. All they needed was a lonely girl."

"You don't look lonely."

"Why should I? It's not becoming." Her head was in her folded arms, on the ground, so that her voice was muffled.

"It's not funny," he said, annoyed. "Lonely is not a fashion!"

"Not always," she said, her shoulders shaking.

"Are you teasing me?" he asked suspiciously. He was frustrated enough without getting laughed at.

For answer, she raised her face. Her eyes were red, and strands of hair were matted across her cheeks, wet from her tears.

Amazed, he stared.

"She was all mine," Barb said. "And now, suddenly, this morning, out of the blue, it's over. Over."

"I thought you knew—"

"No, I didn't know!" she screamed. "I thought *you* knew."

"*Me!* I thought Balook had been tortured or something, afraid of me, afraid of everyone! I chased him—"

"Oh, hell, why fight," she said. "I'm sorry."

"Sorry? For being lonely?"

"For trying to make you admit you knew."

"Admit I—"

"Well, *somebody* knew! Not that it matters, now."

"You mean all that camaraderie—just to—?"

"Pointless, isn't it," she said wryly. "I thought you were putting on an act. I just couldn't keep mine up. I'm not the type."

"The type?"

"Social. With boys—you know."

"I—" He hesitated. "Know."

They found themselves staring at each other with suddenly intense understanding. Both flushed, and looked away, embarrassed.

"Scale knew," Thor said after a moment.

"Who?"

"You said somebody knew about the two *Baluchitheriums*. He—"

"*Baluchitheria.*"

"Do you want to hear this or don't you?" he snapped.

She smiled, abruptly pretty. "I apologize."

She understood about being alone. About needing a friend. She was his age, and a girl. She was like him, in mirror image. That was abruptly appealing.

"You aren't going to tell me?" she asked.

"What?"

She raised her face—her eyes were red . . .

"The man who knew."

"Oh." He had allowed himself to be distracted, foolishly. "Don Scale knew about Balook and Theria. He's our Project Manager. I knew he knew something, but I didn't know what. He knew about the second Project, and didn't tell anyone. If he hadn't been so damned secretive—"

She nodded. "Maybe he thought we wouldn't cooperate if we knew. And maybe we wouldn't have."

"Why not? They could have had the two rhinos together from the start."

"And had them mate early, and maybe die of complications, and ruin the whole thing," she said. "No, I can see keeping them apart. What I can't see is not telling us. What is this—a military secret so that nobody can help anybody else no matter what is wasted in inefficency?"

"I think Mr. Scale has a military background. 'Need to know' and all that."

"Need to know!" she snorted.

"What makes you think they'd mate? Too soon, I mean?"

"Don't you know *anything*? Theria's in heat. Was, anyway. That's why Balook came all that distance. But by the time he got here, she was over it. Just as well, maybe."

In heat. Why hadn't he realized? No wonder Balook had battered down all obstacles! Thor had seen the neighborhood transformed when some animal was in heat. Dogs, cats—the female gave out a smell that carried wherever the wind went, and every male of the species responded. Docile pets became unmanageable, until that odor faded.

So all the pieces had fallen into place. Balook had grown up. Thor was superfluous. So was Barb, as far as Theria went. Nothing they could do could change that. He should have known his life with Balook could not last forever, just as childhood could not last forever. Everyone had to grow up.

He'll be interested in her for days

Still it hurt.

"Have they done it yet?" he asked.

"Done what?"

Was she teasing him, or truly perplexed? "You know. Mated."

"I told you: she was out of heat by the time he got here."

"Which means she might not be interested. But he didn't travel all the way for a cold shoulder. Heat isn't like a switch that suddenly clicks off. He'll be interested in her for days, until the last trace of it is gone."

"I suppose that is the way males are," she said, with a partial smile to show she did not quite mean it. "It does lead to trouble. But no, there hasn't been anything. Yet. I—I think they really don't know how. They might have the urge, but—"

"I have a notion what that's like."

"There's no manual for them. They can't even pick it up from others of their kind."

"Maybe when her next heat comes."

"Maybe. But it may still be too soon for them. I guess the two projects were going to be joined in another year or two, when both were all the way mature. They're like teenagers now."

Teenagers. Like himself and Barb.

She scrambled to her feet, dusting off bits of grass. She seemed recovered from her emotional malaise. "C'mon. We can still be friends."

"What for?" he asked bitterly. "We're just extras now."

"Friends with *them*, I mean." She walked back toward the stable.

She was right. Balook still recognized Thor, and did not run from him now. But when Thor called "Down!" for the rhino to lower his head so the boy could climb up in his massive neck, Balook would not obey. He would not be ridden; he had another interest now.

There was no question of trying to take Balook back to his own ranch. He possessed the rhino stubbornness in full measure. They would have had to drug him and carry him, which would have been an extraordinary task, and he would not have stayed. Balook was here with Theria, and here he would remain. Until he figured out how to do what he had come for.

THOR MOVED INTO a spare cabin on the premises and became part of the Theria Project, for the moment. There seemed to be little point in staying, as the personnel here were fully competent. The gap in the fence was fixed, and the two great rhinos were happy.

But there was Barb. Thor had had little experience

with people his own age, and less with girls. Barb was approachable; she had similar interests—namely, huge extinct animals—and she was pretty. She could carry the conversational ball when he faltered. He was often annoyed at her "C'mon" pushiness, but he liked her. He liked her a lot, and could not say so. He felt the enormous attraction of a girl who truly understood about dedication to animals. Barb would never, ever tease him about Balook. But beyond that, there was a void. He had no better notion what to do about it than Balook did.

"C'mon, let's have a picnic," Barb said one afternoon. "We'll put some hardtack in the bikes and loop out to the lake."

There it was again. She had already set it up, knowing he would go along. He went along, because it was awkward to say no. He would have liked the idea better if *he* had set it up—if he had had the courage to—if he had even thought of it. Which bordered on another irritation: the suspicion that Barb was smarter than he was. He now knew that she was a year younger than he, though she was at his level in school.

They followed the local trails out. Barb's bike was less sophisticated than his, lacking the boosters, but they weren't going cross-country anyway. She pedaled ahead, showing the way, long-legged and energetic. Her curls flopped back and forth in the wind, and her jeans were tight across her rear and thighs. She would not pass for a tomboy much longer. He felt guilty for noticing, but he kept watching.

The lake was beautiful. It was ringed by dark green pines, and the water was glassy clear. Fish leaped occasionally, making sudden splashes. It was exactly the kind of setting Thor had come to love, and it was evident Barb did too. Nature, unspoiled.

Barb spread a cloth over the pine needles and set out sandwiches. Thor saw they were handmade; she had put them together herself. It had probably cost more to buy the makings than it would have to order them whole, but it was her notion of independence. He liked it.

But before they started eating, she looked out over the water. "C'mon, let's go for a swim, work up a proper appetite."

She just couldn't go long without stirring things up! "Can't. No suits."

"Oh." She considered momentarily. "Well, we could—"

"No." He wasn't going to let her tease him into an embarrassing situation.

"No one would see."

"*We* would see," he said, feeling a flush developing: exactly what he had sought to avoid.

"Yes, but we know each other."

Thor turned the idea over in his mind. Its appeal grew, perversely. Why not, after all? He would never have suggested such a thing, but now all he had to do was go along. He had never seen a girl nude. Not a real one. It was bound to be a fascinating experience.

But *she* would see *him*, too . . .

Well, hell. What was the difference? "Okay," he said, his heart pounding in a fashion he hoped didn't show.

"Oh, you're always so stuffy!" she exclaimed.

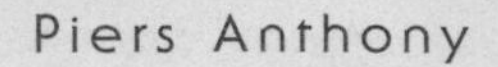

Balook was here with Theria,
and here he would remain

"I said 'Okay'."

"You—" She paused. "You *agreed*?"

"Sure. Do us good to cool off in the water." He knew he would have to hurry, because already the masculine reaction was stirring. If he stripped rapidly and jumped into the cold water before it showed, good enough. Otherwise he'd be in trouble.

She seemed flustered. "But I thought you—"

He caught on. "You thought I wouldn't do it? Why did you suggest it, then?"

"No, I—"

Now he was intrigued, made bold by her hesitation. "So I called your bluff. So let's go swimming!"

"Oh, all right," she said, disgruntled. "You first."

"Ladies first. You suggested it, you know."

"Women are equal now. 'Sposed to be, anyway. You don't have to defer to me. Go ahead. Undress."

She was trying to bluff him out after all. Thor discovered that he was rather enjoying this game. It would have been different with a truly self-possessed girl, but now he knew that Barb had no firmer social base that he did. One part of him was shocked; another part wanted to be naked with Barb. That gave it the lure and threat of the best competition.

"All right, me first, then you," he said, putting his hand to his belt. His masculine reaction was being held in abeyance by the tension of the situation; he could get through if he avoided thinking about it too much.

"Not *here*!" she squealed.

"Here is where we're going to swim, isn't it?"

"Yes, but you don't change in public. Go behind a tree or something."

"I'm *not* changing, I'm undressing. What difference does it make where I do it?" But of course it did make a difference, though he wasn't sure why.

She sighed. "I guess you're right. I started it. Might as well do it here."

Was she trying to bluff him again? He felt as if he were boosting over the lake, heedless of his landing. "Right."

Thor loosened his belt and pulled out his shirt. He took off his shoes and socks. Then he held his breath and let down his trousers. He realized now that it was not the notion of his own undressing that made him react; it was the notion of hers. He would have to head for the water the moment she started.

"Wait!" Barb cried.

Thor paused in his undershorts. "What now?" *Ha!* he thought.

"I can't do it. So I guess you shouldn't, either."

He had won, but he was disappointed. Having come this close to doing something he had thought he could not, something he might remember for the rest of his life, he preferred to seize the moment and go all the way. "Come on, Barb—let's do it. No one will know."

"It's not what you think," she said miserably. "I'm not a prude. I really would like to swim. Swim with you, I mean. I just can't."

"Okay," he said, embarrassed for her. He had pushed it too far, he realized. He pulled up his trousers. "Forget it."

"No, I've always been honest. Not popular, but honest. I'll tell you exactly why. It's because I'm—I'm not developed. Yet. I'm fourteen, and behind in my—it just takes longer for some girls—"

"I said forget it!" This was too complete a victory.

"I look like hell in a bathing suit, and worse nude. I don't want you to see me—"

"It's *okay*, Barb. I was just bluffing, myself."

"I don't think so. Not at the end."

"And you're not—" He hesitated, at a loss for a socially acceptable way to phrase it. "Your—your legs look nice, and—"

She glanced down at herself. "I guess I'm starting low and working up," she agreed. Her gaze stopped at her chest. "My—they haven't—"

"It doesn't matter. Let's eat."

"Next year I won't have to be ashamed. I—"

"For God's sake, *stop* it!" he shouted. "I *understand*! I'm no Adonis myself."

"I don't think you do, quite." She was blushing harder. "I want to look good—for you. Because you're the only, you know, the rhinos. And a decent person. I don't want you to have a bad image of me."

Again, Thor had mixed emotions. Her confessional candor embarrassed him, but he was deeply flattered and gratified by her feeling. It was Barb's way to tease him with banter or provocative remarks, then suddenly drop into some expression of true emotion. Perhaps it was her way of working up to something serious. But he found it awkward to cope with. She would put him in one mood, then hit him with material for another mood. This confession of hers had abolished his resentment of her ready wit; she was just as vulnerable as he, and needed that wit to compensate. The fact that she liked him enough to tell him her shame stirred him as strongly as the thought of her nudity had, but at a more fundamental level. They were hovering at the brink of something serious.

He wanted to kiss her, but the situation was wrong. He knew that the wrong move now could turn her ferociously against him. He had to play it carefully, so that his own social clumsiness would not destroy their relationship. "Why don't we make a date for next year?" he asked. "Same place. Same—you know. If we want to."

"It's a date!" she exclaimed, abruptly smiling. "Same uniform." She had found the word he lacked.

Thor nodded, tremendously relieved. He had succeeded in navigating the rapids and holding on to the

gains they had made in their relationship. It was already clear that they were meant for each other; their shared isolation from others and their community of interest with the Projects had perhaps made that inevitable. But they were both too young to handle the full experience, as with Balook and Theria.

"Wait!" Barb cried

The truth was, Barb's nudity could have shown him little that her clothing had not already betrayed. She had a pretty face and a good mind, but portions of her body just had not yet done their thing.

He climbed back into the rest of his clothing. He had, at least, learned how much she liked him. That was well worthwhile. The heavy beating of his heart had settled into a warm heat in his chest. There were ways in which this was better than the nudity would have been. She had bared her feelings instead of her body.

She pushed a sandwich at him. "Wouldn't it be simple if people just went in heat, like the animals. No worry, no concern, no talking—just give with the smell and it's done!"

The idea appalled him. "People—in heat!"

"Well, it makes life easier for the animals."

"Who wants that kind of simplicity! Anyway, they haven't—"

"But they will, maybe next cycle."

"Yeah. And next year we'll swim."

She shrugged, relaxed again. She had in effect recovered her emotional clothing, and was back in charge. "You know, Balook and Theria are about our age, in rhino terms, I think. Do you think they'll have a calf?"

The parallel bothered him. "No way to know. They were both androids—created animals. They might be sterile, like mules."

"Only one way to find out," she said.

"Yes, let them try it and see."

"That's what they'll be doing." She looked about.

In the course of their conversation they had finished eating. "Well, let's go home."

But they had forgotten that this was a scheduled rain afternoon, and they both got soaked. They might as well have gone swimming in their clothes.

"WE CAN'T EXTEND it any more, lad," Skip said apologetically. "Now that Balook's moved out, you'll have to go back to regular school. No more waivers."

Thor turned away from the TV phone. He had known that the Department of Education would catch up with him sometime. Barb retained her waiver, because the *Baluchitheria* were here, but Thor was officially out of work.

He had no choice. He had to go home.

He packed his things and put them in the car. It was programmed for the other Project; all he had to do was get in. But first he had to say farewell to Balook.

It was impossible, he thought as he walked. He had known Balook practically all of Balook's life. They had been inseparable, in sickness and in health. How could Balook desert him now?

Maybe if he called to the rhino, reminded him . . .

The animals were in the giant stable, standing side by side. They were not confined there; indeed, they would have broken out if they felt squeezed. They merely preferred it to the bright sun. In the evening they would meander out to crop the forest-top. They did not seem to sleep very much, but of course it could be hard to tell, because they were capable of settling by a big tree and eating its leaves in their sleep.

"Balook!" Thor called, walking up behind.

There was no response.

"Balook! I'm going back to the Project. *Our* Project," Thor said.

Balook leaned over and nudged Theria with his bent nose.

Thor remembered how the animal had suffered when left alone as a calf. Now he was not alone, and those years of human association seemed to mean nothing.

"Balook!" Thor stood beside the pillarlike foreleg, his head not even reaching the junction of leg with body. He was impressed, as he had been so often before, with the sheer mass of Balook's parts. Even to call this limb "elephantine" was a misnomer, for no elephant had a leg this large.

Thor put his hand on the tremendous knee. The skin hung loosely here, like the folds of a heavy leather jacket. Above it there was sparse hair. Modern rhinos had little hair, but *Baluchitherium* was of more primitive stock. Thor liked Balook better this way; he would have looked naked without his fur.

Naked . . . He remembered the afternoon with Barb. Maybe if human beings had retained thicker body fur, they would not be so sensitive about exposure of their torsos. Yet that exposure could be exciting, too. Now he wished they had indulged themselves in that swim; he thought about it often, and sometimes dreamed about it. In retrospect it seemed like a phenomenal opportunity squandered.

That failure mirrored this one with the rhino. Closeness denied. "Balook," he said once more, pinching a handful of the heavy skin.

Balook only shook his skin in the way that animals could, as if to dislodge a stinging fly.

Something snapped. "*Damn* you!" Thor cried, insulted. He made a fist and struck the leg as hard as he could.

"I saw that!" Barb exclaimed, standing in the entranceway. "You hit him! You hit Balook!"

"I'll hit him again!" Thor shouted, blinded by rage. "The ungrateful slob!"

Balook had not even seemed to notice the blow, and it was obvious that nothing Thor could do could harm the animal. Those great legs routinely knocked sizable branches from trees. But Barb was outraged. She ran up and grabbed Thor's arm. "Get away from him, you monster!"

Thor, maddened by the hindrance, threw her aside. It was not unconscious; he reacted to her as an aspect of the animal's betrayal, and flailed against it. *She* was part of it, and he was losing her association as surely as Balook's. The burgeoning feeling he had for her inverted and became black wrath. He knew it was wrong of him to react this way, and was horrified, but still he did it.

Barb stumbled into Balook's leg herself, but also hung on to Thor's arm. She was no fainting female, but a healthy and committed person. Thor tried to shake her loose. She slid farther down, still clutching his arm—and she bit him.

The sudden pain sobered him. Thor was free, now—but it was too late to make amends. Not with Barb, the way she was.

"Get out of here!" Barb screamed, slumping on Balook's foot, her face against one of the three enormous hoof-toes. "Go away! Don't ever come back!" Her rage was as ferocious as his, but it had more justice.

Thor got out. It was over. Not only Balook—but Barb. Before it had started, really. He didn't even know what to feel.

IT LAY DEAD: white, fluffy, and innocent. "I'm glad for you, fella," Thor said. He picked it up, looking at each head in turn. It was a rabbit, with the head and forepaws tapering into a round body—whose posterior was another head and forepaws facing the other way. It had no hind legs, no bunny-tail. It had lived a normal rabbit span in an abnormal manner. With no regular means to eliminate bladder or bowel refuse, it had had to vomit out whatever remained in its gut, whenever the toxic level became too great. Eat, digest, vomit; eat, digest, vomit. It had urinated through a tube set in its belly, implanted there surgically just after its grotesque "birth."

Life had been torture for this creature, but the law had required the Project to maintain its existence as long as possible. Thor had watched it slowly decline, and shared the agony of its tedious terminal illness. How much better for it, if it had never lived!

And who was responsible for its life in this state? Thor himself was, to a degree, for he was part of the Project, supporting its researches. That guilt never quite left his awareness. He had tried to ease it by devising cute names for the uncute creatures, such as Pushmi-Pullyu for this one, but had known all along that one swift smash at each head would have served the creature in better stead.

He put the emaciated body in a freezer locker, and made a note on the record card: precise time of expiration. He went to the next hutch.

Pooh, the miniature bear, looked alertly up at him. Thor reached in and picked up the creature; it stood some twenty centimeters tall at the shoulders and weighed only a few kilograms: the size of an average cat. It was friendly, because Thor had befriended it. But for the secrecy regulations, it could have been given to some family as a pet. Instead, it spent its time in this bleak cage, lonely.

Lonely. How well Thor understood! He glanced at his right forearm, where the faint scars of teeth marks showed. Barb's bite, not serious physically, but horrendous emotionally. They marked the onset of his own loneliness.

Holding the tiny bear, stroking its fine fur, Thor thought of Balook. After almost two years, the memory still hurt. One sniff of that female, and the big lummox of a rhino had walked out of Thor's life forever.

Oh, there had been contacts. Barb had phoned several times, but Thor had refused the calls. Talking with her would only have made it worse; better for both of them to let it die.

Pushmi-Pullyu

After a while she had sent letters. He had a little pile of them on his desk, unopened, unanswered. He couldn't bring himself to destroy them, so they just sat there, mute reminders of his loss.

It had been especially bad after the first year—the time they would have had their date to go swimming, nude. He wondered what she looked like, now. She had probably forgotten all about that date. He hadn't—but he hadn't kept it.

Instead he had gotten involved in what remained of the Project, here: the freak zoo. He had learned how to care for the forlorn creatures here. These would never leave him; they couldn't. Except by dying. Like the Pushmi-Pullyu bunny.

He carried Pooh with him as he continued his rounds. The little thing needed every bit of comfort it could get, and it was never any trouble. A real bear might have been ornery and unmanageable, but this one's personality differed from the large wild ursines as much as Balook's nature differed from wild rhinos.

There it was again. He could not forget Balook. These animals of the zoo needed him as much as Balook ever had, and more than Balook did now—but it wasn't the same. Balook had not only needed him; *he* had needed Balook. He had not deserted the rhino, the rhino had deserted him.

Now he entered the invertebrate section: cool, damp pits for experimental boneless animals. He let Sluggo out for a slide around the interior garden. The monstrous two meter long slug moved with respectable velocity, about two kilometers per hour under full steam. But it had too many reflexes of its smaller cousins, and thought it could ascend vertical walls. It could not; size made a difference, and it was confined to the level. But it would hurt itself trying, if he didn't watch it.

Thor checked the toothed worm. To do this, he had to pour water on its patch of soil, forcing it to come up for air. If it didn't rise within a minute, he would have to dig it out. It might be dying, or merely balky; it was his job to be certain it was all right.

It came up, the ring of teeth clattering angrily. Those teeth could abrade rock, but progress was so slow it wasn't worth it. So Wormgear was a failure—like the rest of the inmates here. No fault of its own.

"Sluggo! Get down!" Thor yelled as the slug nosed into the retaining wall. Too late; the sticky slime gave way and the creature fell over on its back, squirming.

Thor hurried over, pushing at the spongy hide with his foot. This was not queasiness on his part; he was

"Sluggo! Get down!"

still holding Pooh and didn't dare put him down in this region. Also, the slime on Sluggo's skin was an irritant to human skin; gloves had to be worn for handling. Finally, he had more power in his foot, and it took power to roll Sluggo over, for he weighed almost two hundred kilograms.

Thor pushed, and Sluggo twisted, and slowly, together, they got the slug on his underside. There did not seem to be any damage, this time; the fall had been short, no more than half a meter, and Sluggo's body was resilient. "Now watch your step!" Thor said reprovingly. "You can go back in your cell for the day, you know."

The slug paid no attention. It was big, not bright, and Thor wasn't sure it could hear him. It had eyestalks, but they did not project far because of the inhibition of gravity, and probably touch was the main sense that guided it. No slug this size could function like an ordinary one; the liabilities of scale made it impossible. Without a controlled environment and special food this one would soon have expired. For all that, Thor rather liked Sluggo; the creature was quiet and not at all vicious.

The same could not be said for Dino, in the next section. Dino looked like a dinosaur, with large scales all over his body, but he was a mammal. He was derived from the pangolin, the scaled mammal, but was much larger. He stood Thor's height, and walked on two hind legs, and he would have eaten Thor and all the other denizens of the zoo if he had the opportunity.

Still, Thor liked Dino too. The animal was no more responsible for his condition than any of the others were, and illustrated the other side of the project—and of man's nature. For every sweet-tempered creature like Pooh, a nasty brute like Dino. Each showed his true feelings, and each was reflected in Thor's own inner passions.

"Thor!"

He turned. It was Skip, now also active at the zoo. Without Balook, it was that or dismissal. "Trouble?"

"Could be. Call from the Western Project. For you."

"You know I don't take those calls!" He was locked in that prison of his own making, and hated it, but could not escape.

"It's not her," Skip said compassionately. "It's the boss. And he's serious. You'd better hop to it, lad."

Thor sighed. "Take Pooh." He handed over the tiny bear and went to the office to answer the phone. He could not refuse a call from authority; not if he wanted to keep his job.

It was the Project Manager, Don Scale's counterpart at the Theria Project. He was a portly, serious man, not given to minor pleasantries. "Nemmen, we need you."

Thor looked at the image in the screen, surprised. "How so, Mr. Duke?"

"The Baluchitherium Project is being cut back. We're low on funds now, and next year will be worse. We have to take measures."

That figured. Now that Balook and Theria had proved it could be done, governmental interest was waning. The significance of the successful re-creation of an extinct species was phenomenal, but now those perfected techniques were being applied to other things. Super-beef, super-hens, super-fish—the livestock problem was being solved by manufactured breeds. Even super-rats, useful for reducing certain types of garbage efficiently. Balook

Dino looked like a dinosaur

was merely one stage in a long chain; he was no longer needed. As far as the government was concerned, he could relapse back into extinction.

"Measures," Thor echoed as these thoughts flowed through his mind.

"We're faced with the necessity to cut down on equipment and personnel."

That sent a shock through Thor. Now he appreciated

the relevance! He was about to lose his job! "I—understand, sir," he said, dry-mouthed.

"We're closing down the Western Project, as it is largely cropped out now. It was never intended for continuous forage by two adult animals. We'll move them to the Eastern Project."

"But it's not in shape!" Thor protested. "The stable's been dismantled, the personnel are gone—"

"We have sold the Western Premises to a developer for a large apartment complex. It's prime land in a good zone. The funds will be used to renovate the Eastern facilities."

"Oh." That was Duke's way of saying that the Project had made an excellent business deal, and had money to use. The government, in its bureaucratic fashion, probably would not realize what had been done until too late to pre-empt the money. Projects, like laboratory animals, had to fend for themselves at times. "But where do I come in?" For he was evidently not to be fired after all.

"You know how to mount and ride one of the animals. It is necessary to walk them across."

"Oh," Thor repeated. "Well, I'm not volunteering."

"Naturally not," Duke said. "You are being assigned. You have two hours to organize your affairs; the car has already been dispatched."

"Now wait a minute!" Thor protested.

Duke met his gaze, unperturbed. "You do wish to retain employment, Mr. Nemmen?" He faded out, certain of the answer. He was a man who got things done.

Thor started an angry retort anyway, but knew it

would have been futile even had he remained connected. Mr. Duke did not joke; what he said, he meant. He was not in Thor's direct line of command, but he could have Thor fired. And would, if he saw the need.

Ah, well. Now that he was committed, Thor discovered that he was relieved. He wanted to see Balook again—and Barb. For two years he had tried to deny this; he could do so no longer. Even though both would probably meet him with contempt.

"I'M SORRY FOR what I said to you," Barb's first letter said. "I didn't mean it. I mean I *did*, then, but when I cooled down and thought about it, I realized how you must feel. There was this time when Theria kept doing something, I don't even remember what, now, but it made me so darned *mad* I finally hit her on the knee. I hurt my hand and she didn't even feel it, but I felt so guilty! I guess that was what made me overreact when I saw you do it. It was myself I was mad at, more than you. I was yelling at the part of myself I hated. I wish I had understood, before I opened my mouth. I know you love Balook, and hated to leave him, and it just overflowed. It's exactly the way I am, too.

"Please call me . . ."

Thor set the sheet down, his vision blurring. He had never answered, of course, because he had never opened the letter. If she had apologized to him in the first letter, what had she done in the later ones?

He had only an hour left, and he was supposed to be getting his things in order. But at the moment it was more important to get his mind in order. He had to know what Barb had been saying to him, before he saw

Cute names for uncute creatures

her again. If only to assess the depth of his guilt.

He nerved himself and opened the next, scanning down its lines. She expressed hope that he would at least write back to her, even if he didn't forgive her for her intemperate outburst. Then: "Balook stands forlornly in the corner of the pasture, facing east. Theria's long out of heat, now, and things are back to normal, so I guess he has time to think. We have to remember that they are animals; they can't handle more than one important notion at a time. When Theria was in heat, or in the last stages of it, Balook just couldn't be bothered with anything else. It wasn't that he didn't care, just that for him it would be like one of us trying to solve a trigonometric problem in the head while reciting Shakespeare aloud on stage. He just couldn't do it. But now it's different, and he remembers. Balook misses you terribly . . ."

And Thor hadn't even answered. Hadn't even *known*, thanks to his oikheaded refusal to read her words. His guilt was worse than even his projections of it!

He went to the last of the six letters. ". . . I guess I've alienated you, and I can't blame you. Maybe you're burning these letters without reading them. So I won't bother you any more. I'll just say, for the last time, that if you ever change your mind, the door is always open. Balook loves you, and I'd like to, if." There was no ellipsis, no further qualification; her implication was left as open as the offer.

If he ever came to his senses.

He was seventeen years old, too old to cry. It made no difference. Blindly, he jammed the letters into a pocket. What was the use? He would face the music soon enough!

A comely young woman came out to meet the car. Thor scowled. The Project was not yet out of funds, he thought, if it could afford such decorative secretaries. This was definitely the Project, though details had changed; he could tell by the distinctive rhino odor, that brought back so many memories.

"Hello, Thor," she said.

He looked at her again. Her brown hair was tied back in a neat bun, and she was immaculately dressed in a conservative gray blouse and black skirt and small gray shoes. Probably she had been given his name on a routing slip. He did not like being treated like baggage. "Have we met before?" he asked somewhat coldly.

"Thor, you broke our date!" she said severely.

"Lady, I don't know what—" He paused, the realization belatedly dawning. "Barb!"

"Idiot!" she said. "You didn't recognize me!"

He considered her a third time. "You've changed." An understatement! Two years had wrought far more physical change in her than they had in him. She was sixteen now, and had been transformed. The lanky angles had been replaced by thoroughly feminine curves, and her face had matured subtly. She had been pretty before; now she was beautiful.

It was like meeting a stranger. Worse, perhaps, because this was a stranger who knew him. There was no parity in the relationship.

"C'mon, I'll show you your room," she said. And suddenly she seemed familiar again. The professional young woman showed as a veneer covering the same girl. That made him feel better.

She hardly gave him time to set down his bag before she had him out in the stable. "Wait till you see!"

"See what?"

"It." She smiled knowingly.

First he saw Balook. No, not Balook—this was Theria, standing as tall as Balook had before. And beside her, almost beneath her, stood a tiny, big-headed, long-legged thing that could not have weighed more than a hundred kilograms.

"They made it!" Thor exclaimed.

"Yes, and she calved," Barb said proudly.

She put her hand on the calf's head. "We saved him as a surprise for you. Isn't he darling?"

"Yes." Thor's throat was tight. It was like seeing Balook again, that first time, eight years before. The rhinos had successfully mated; *Baluchitherium* was now a viable contemporary species. But all that seemed unimportant at the moment; what counted now was the reality of this ungainly calf. *This* one would never be lonely!

"You're wonderful, Blooky," Barb said, putting her arms around the calf. The humped nose nuzzled her face.

Thor watched, still remembering his first experience with Balook. By human standards, the creature was ugly, with great folds of skin and a misshapen body. But obviously Barb considered it beautiful, and that made her beautiful, quite apart from her other attributes. He knew it again: there could be no other woman for him. What a fool he had been to cut her off these two years!

"You can touch him," she said. "He knows that anyone his mother tolerates is okay, and she knows anyone *I* tolerate is okay." She leaned down to kiss its wrinkled snout. "Isn't that so, Blooky!"

Thor reached out cautiously to stroke the sparse fur. "Yes," he repeated. If he had only known!

"Here's Balook!" Barb said brightly, glancing up.

Now he showed in silhouette in the giant doorway: twelve tons of superbly powerful rhino, almost six meters tall at the shoulder. The most majestic land-walking animal to tread the earth since the dinosaurs passed from the scene. Absolutely beautiful. Balook!

Would the huge rhino remember him? Thor stepped forward uncertainly, awed by this creature three times his height and well over a hundred times his mass. "Balook . . ." he said.

The lofty head descended. The small eyes peered. The monstrous nose came close, like the scoop of a steam shovel. It touched Thor, sniffing. The large, mobile lips quivered. The ears, far back on the skull, twitched.

Thor stood still. He was not afraid, though he knew that one twitch of that colossal nose could hurl him through the wall. His apprehension was emotional: was he friend or stranger?

Balook's head moved. The side of his jaw nudged Thor's hip. It was a familiar gesture, Balook's way of saying "I will pick you up."

"You remember!" Thor cried, throwing his arms around Balook's nose, as far as they would reach. The head was a meter and a half long, far more massive than Thor's whole body. "Oh, Balook!"

Suddenly he was in the air, dangling precariously as the head went up. Thor scrambled to catch hold of the ears, getting the anchorage he needed to save himself a six meter fall. His knees were clamped over Balook's two eyes. There was no harm there; the rhino's eyelids were so tough that only a deliberate kick would hurt, and sight was not his most important sense. "Oh, Balook!" Thor repeated joyfully, two miserable years vanished.

Thor dug his toes into the available crevices of the rhino's massive skull, grabbed a double handful of heavy skin on the neck, and squirmed about to bestride the neck, facing forward. His good traveling clothes were getting creased and soiled, but he didn't care. It was just like old times!

"You look a sight!" Barb called.

"A happy sight!" he called back.

She turned away. He wasn't sure why. She couldn't be jealous of his restored rapport with Balook. Maybe it was that she was too formally dressed to do the same with Theria at the moment.

SO THEY WERE reunited, and more, for now Balook had a family, and Thor was part of it, like an uncle. It was not that the rhino didn't care who played with his calf; the approach of any stranger, human or animal, brought a warning snort, and ominous stomping of the heavy feet. These were signals it was wise to heed. Balook's attitude had matured with his body and status; now he was dangerous in the way that any bull or stag was, when crossed.

Thor was riding Balook once when a stray dog came

near, and he felt the muscles of the rhino's powerful shoulders tense. The compound was not tight; small animals like dogs could squeeze through gaps and sneak in to raid the food. These were tolerated as long as they kept their place. But this dog looked at Blooky, and Balook was abruptly taut. Suddenly Thor was made aware of the juggernaut of destruction that this animal could become when aroused. Balook was still gentle, but now it was a selective gentleness, complemented by a new male pride. Push him the wrong way, and Balook would fight—and there was nothing living that could conceivably stand against him.

The dog took the warning and hurried away, though Balook had never moved. Animals often understood each other in ways that human beings did not. Had Thor not been in close physical contact at the time, he would not have known of the interchange. But it was genuine; had the dog made a single threatening gesture toward Blooky, he would have been in instant peril for his life.

Abruptly it was clear why Thor had been summoned. He could control Balook; no one else could. Balook might have followed where Theria, guided by Barb, led—but that was by no means certain. On the grounds of the Project it didn't matter; this was a controlled environment. On a trek between locations—potential disaster.

Of course it was stretching things to believe that Thor controlled Balook. Even in the old days, Thor had only guided the rhino. It was a perpetual game Balook had loved to play. But he had always had a mind of his own, and on occasion asserted it. Now that assertion was stronger. But Balook still did accept Thor's guidance, when there were no conflict. Now that the imperatives of mating and fatherhood had been honored, Balook was satisfied to be with Thor again. Thor remembered Barb's comment in the letter: how Balook had stood for hours at a time in the pasture, facing east. The bond between them had never been sundered; Thor had merely denied it for a time, to his shame.

If Balook had forgiven Thor his absence, Barb had not. She hardly spoke to him now. She had been open at the start, but then shut down. The way she had turned away from him—now he understood. She had done her duty by welcoming him back to the Project, introducing him to Blooky, and seeing him reunited with Balook. She owed him no more. Thor could not argue with that; he knew he deserved it. In a way he was glad; it gave him more of a chance to get used to her as she was now. Oh, it stung; but it was right. Once he worked his way back into her favor the hard way, he would know it was genuine. Perhaps the effort would allow him to expiate some of his guilt.

The process of closing down the site went on, while little Blooky gained his walking legs. Thor and Barb took turns exercising the baby rhino. This might have led to pleasant contacts and increasing intimacy between the two human beings, but Barb rebuffed any overtures Thor made. In fact she sniped at him with increasing rancor, for decreasing reason.

Thor was irritated, but he was older than he had been, and he had a better basis for understanding. Two years ago he had lost his rhino, and Barb had kept them both. He had been frustrated and unreasonable. Now

Barb was losing Theria, and Thor was gaining the entire family. Jealousy, loss, despair—whatever it was, Thor well understood it. He had traveled the full course himself, isolating himself until forcibly drawn back by events. Balook was being restored to him, through no virtue of Thor's. He was in no position to judge her.

He understood—but still it wasn't fun, having Barb continually at his throat. She was an attractive girl, more than attractive, with a lot to offer—everything to offer. He had to work with her. She had tried to reach him while he sulked, before; now he had to try to reach her.

"Barb," he called one day as she brought Blooky back from his circuit. "C'mon, let's talk!"

"Don't get smart!" she snapped.

"Look—I know I was a heel to refuse your calls and not to read your letters. I was mad. I don't blame you. But we've got to work together now."

"Sure," she said acidly. "Just like that!"

"I know how you feel. I felt that way for two years. Please—I apologize for the way I was. I was a freak! I'm *sorry*."

"*You're* sorry!"

"Let's go out to the lake and talk."

"And skinny-dip. You'd like that!"

Thor considered. "Yes, I suppose I would."

She turned away. "Forget it!"

He caught hold of her arm. "I don't care *where* we talk! Just so we get this straightened out. We can't—"

Barb whirled, her free hand swinging up. She slapped him across the cheek.

It was no weak stroke. She was a vigorous, healthy girl, as she had always been, accustomed to brushing down *Baluchitheria* and hoisting herself on Theria's back. Thor's head rocked back, and for a moment he saw red. He was surprised to discover that there really was an optical effect; it was not merely poetic license.

But he was older than he had been, and had learned the futility of violence. He grabbed her again, turned her about to face him, and pulled her close. She struggled, but he had grown a bit physically too, and was stronger. She lifted her hand to strike him again—but before she completed the motion, he kissed her.

For a moment she was stunned, unresponsive. But only a moment. Then she reacted. She shoved him violently away.

"Of all the nerve!" she cried. "What do you think you're doing?"

"Something I've wanted to do for two years," he said soberly. "Only I didn't know it."

"You think I'm going to play up to you just because you've got them all now!" she said furiously. "All the Balooks!"

"No, I—"

"You think I'm in heat or something, and—"

"No!"

"You've got the rhinos but you're not satisfied! You want everything!"

Now it was coming into the open. She was jealous in the same way he had been, and was close to admitting it. "I guess I do," he said. "I thought all I wanted was Balook, but now—"

"One amateurish kiss!" she snorted disdainfully.

"I sort of hoped you'd like me a little for myself," he said. "I think you're a great girl, and I wish I'd answered your—"

"Oh, shut up!" She took Blooky and marched off.

Thor shook his head. "You sure are pretty when you're mad," he muttered inaudibly. "You're pretty anytime!"

Perhaps the kiss hadn't shown Barb anything, but it had shown *him* something. Thor had never been in love—not with a human being—but suddenly it was easy to imagine the condition.

Except that it was obviously a one-sided sentiment.

THINGS WERE NOT perfect between the rhinos, either. Now that Thor had opportunity to work closely with all three of them, he saw that there were times when they got snappish with each other. When Blooky became too venturesome, Theria would nip him so it hurt. He would go crying to Balook, in his fashion playing one parent off against the other.

All three of them seemed fussier than they should be. Thor wasn't certain whether this was because the stress of the incipient move was communicated to them, or whether it was simply that they had some empathy for the problem between him and Barb. If it was the former, there was little that could be done; if the latter, then it was another reason to straighten things out.

But it did require two to straighten. Thor himself had been foolishly adamant for two years; evidently it was an example Barb intended to follow. He wished she was not so like him, in this respect! But he could hardly condemn her for it.

Next day Barb came to him. Her hair was loose, her tresses longer and less curly than they had been two years before. She wore close-fitting blue jeans and a bright green halter. It was obvious that she suffered no embarrassment of underdevelopment any more. "I'll go to the lake, now," she said tightly.

Thor realized that this constituted an apology. He was more than ready to accept it. "We don't have to go there," he said. "All I want is to see you smile."

She looked at him, her brows furrowed. "You've changed."

"I guess I have," he agreed, thinking of the creatures he had seen in the freak zoo. What was Pooh doing now? The bear would be well cared for, of course, but surely it missed Thor. His loyalties had become to a degree divided. Balook was not the only animal that required companionship. "I have suffered for my attitude. I brought it on myself; I know that. I don't want to do that any more. There is too much unavoidable suffering already."

"Sometimes I dream—daydream—about Theria," she said, changing thoughts as was her way. "I go into some kind of trance, and it's as though she and I go home. Home to the Miocene Epoch, I mean: *her* home. I see the animals as her kind knew them, maybe twenty million years ago. It's all—" She shrugged. "Then I come out of it, and I'm so sad."

"Me too," he said. "It was a better world, in its way. No people, no freaks."

"I never did go in for pro-style romance," she said. "I'm sort of amateur myself." Then she smiled, and it was well worth it.

They were friends again.

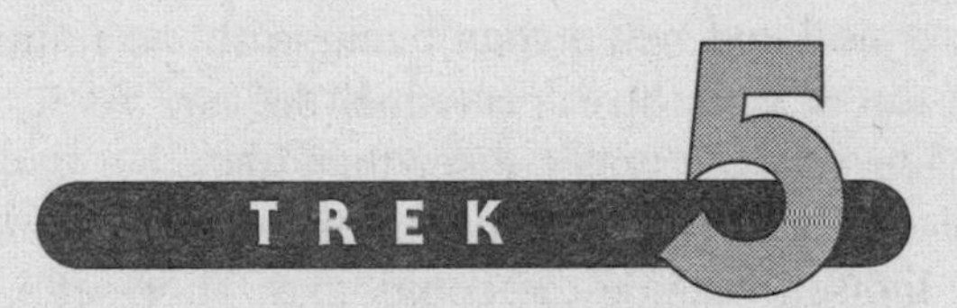

AT LAST THE trek began. They rode astride the giants, guiding them on what was to be a five hundred kilometer haul. Thor was on Balook, Barb on Theria, with baby Blooky tagging along behind his mother. It was Blooky they were most concerned about; the little rhino was small enough to carry on a truck, but would not leave his mother for any extended period. The hustle and bustle of the trek excited him, making him stay closer than usual to Theria. Theria, like Balook, distrusted machinery.

They could have drugged Blooky and trucked him across in a few hours. But Theria's journey would require several days, and she was not about to let her calf go that long. When she became upset, so did Balook. Whereas Theria could balk when annoyed, Balook was liable to attack. So it was essential that the rhinos be kept satisfied, and the entourage was limited by Blooky's pace. The grown animals would have to be given foraging time in the evenings, too; they existed mainly on high green leaves and twigs, and ate hugely.

All of which meant a long, slow journey, with many rests. Thor looked forward to it, because there was nothing he liked better than being with the rhinos and Barb; the other Project personnel did not. As it turned out, their wisdom was greater than his.

Balook led the way, stepping out as though proud to show himself outside the compound. Thor perched lazily on the massive shoulder, every bit as proud. The route had been carefully planned, and a yellow line had been painted on the ground to make quite sure no one got lost. A billion dollars had been invested in the *Baluchitherium* family; no one wanted to expose the rhinos to any unnecessary hazards.

Thor waved to Barb, and she waved back. The other Project personnel stood behind; they could not come with the animals because Balook and Theria were not so tolerant of them. They normally did routine work *around* the rhinos: when the rhinos were in other areas of the compound. When one had to approach an animal directly, Thor or Barb served as escorts, even for the vet. It would be pointless to have others along on the trek; they would serve only to aggravate the rhinos. This was just the five of them: two human, three *Baluchitherium.*

As soon as they cleared the compound, Balook swerved to nibble foliage. "Uh-uh!" Thor said, nudging the neck with a knee. "There's no end to that, and you know it! Keep moving."

Balook made a little grumbling snort, and his back muscles tensed. But he returned to the yellow line. He knew the rules of this game. The relationship between them was not that of master and servant, it was more like weak and strong, with the latter humoring the former. Balook wanted Thor to be happy, perhaps concerned that he might disappear for another two years if affronted. So Balook made small sacrifices, however nonsensical they seemed. Such as passing up perfectly good greenery in order to walk along a barren path.

That was why Thor had had to come. Balook would not have obliged anyone else. As the male, Balook had to lead; Theria would follow him. But even Barb could not have controlled Balook; she had not associated with him during those critical formative years. He would tolerate her as a rider, but would not obey her.

The pace was measured. What a contrast to the headlong rush toward this site, two years before!

BLOOKY HELD UP well, the first day, and by nightfall they had progressed thirty kilometers. A good start!

They camped in a forested region with a clean stream, marked by the Project personnel for this purpose. The stream was vital, for the rhinos had a huge thirst after exertion. Everything was perfect, so far. The worries of Mr. Duke seemed groundless.

Thor and Barb ate supper from their packs, washed in the stream, and settled down in warm sleeping bags next to Blooky. The big animals were out foraging; Blooky, too small to reach the edible treetops, lived mostly on Theria's milk. He eagerly accepted tidbits from their supplies, but this was more entertainment than sustenance for him. So Blooky lay down and relaxed, happy to have company.

"That's why they tolerate us," Barb murmured. "We're baby-sitters."

Thor chuckled. "There's no better job." Indeed, it was a significant signal of trust on the part of the adult animals; they would never have left Blooky alone unguarded, but knew that the human beings would guard him. That freed them to forage and sleep at night, and therefore to travel by day. Had any other human beings been present, they would not have done so. Thor knew that the personnel of the Project were keeping anxious track from a distance, unable to participate. Traffic had been rerouted and the local folk warned away; this trek was to be as isolated as possible. If any creature, human or animal, approached in the dark, Balook and Theria would close right in; they were browsing but alert, and they could both hear and smell very well. They could see well, too, at night—perhaps better than they could by day.

Blooky, aroused by their voices, came over to nuzzle Barb. She reached her arms up to encircle his head. "Yeah, you big baby!" she murmured. "You get your rest; we've a long way to go tomorrow!"

"Say—are you giving out free hugs?" Thor asked.

"Only to babies."

Thor gazed up at the dark sky. The *Baluchitherium* family had brought him and Barb together, and that was all that kept them together. Maybe if he had not sulked for two years, he would now be in a position to associate with Barb on his own merits. He had brought it on himself. She was being polite to him, working with him, but showed no inclination to be more than friends. "I guess I was one," he muttered disconsolately.

Blooky came over to nuzzle Barb

There was a pause. He was afraid she had heard, and that he had angered her again. He wished he could apologize for those two years, but he couldn't, because he had already done so, and it would seem like belaboring a point. He cursed himself yet again for his past intransigence.

"Maybe we'll pass a lake," Barb said.

A lake! Thor remembered their ancient date to go swimming. Was it still on? The more he thought about it, the less he dared inquire. There was no doubt that

Barb's prior objection no longer applied; she had certainly filled out.

"Because you certainly need washing off," she continued.

What? He remained tongue-tied.

"You have dirt all over your face."

Thor surreptitiously felt his guilty face.

"And on your fur, Blooky," she concluded. "Now get to sleep."

Thor blushed in the night. She had been talking to the rhino all the time!

NEXT DAY THEY had to cross a major highway—and they had a surprise. A score of curious people had collected to watch the passage of the great animals. Their bicycles were parked on either side, and more were pedaling in. This was not supposed to happen; these must be ones who were deliberately violating the guideline, and had sneaked by the authorities.

Balook tensed up immediately, not liking the strangers. "Easy, Balook!" Thor said, patting the neck. "I don't like them either, but they're harmless."

Balook relaxed. Thor was not sure whether his words had the effect, or whether the animal was responding to Thor's empathy. Perhaps if Thor was angry, Balook didn't have to be; the situation was under control.

In a minute they were across, Blooky walking between the two grown rhinos, shielded from the spectators. They plunged into the brush, leaving the people behind. There had been no incident, but this was clear warning.

"We've got to keep the crossings clear of people,"

Thor called to Barb. "Balook was ready to bolt; he doesn't like them."

"Right. I'll radio Mr. Duke." She put through the call immediately on her mobile unit.

After a dialogue with the Project Manager, Barb was grim. "They didn't anticipate this, Thor," she said. "They planned the most direct route that included enough suitable forest. But they can't police every meter of it, and where they don't, the gawkers can get in. Somehow news of this trek has spread to everybody despite the news blackout. That yellow line shows them exactly where we'll pass."

"We need that line," Thor said. "Balook is following it; it's a game to him. And I sure wouldn't know the route without it."

"There's a thirty kilo stretch along a truckway," she continued. "They'll cordon it off, but it's too late to change it. And we'll pass right through the center of one town."

"The center of a town!" Thor yelped.

"It has to do with the conjunction of a rail line with a large river; impassable for them and impossible for Blooky. A detour would avoid that but get us into worse development. So we have to use the town, where they have a multi-level tunnel big enough for—"

"A tunnel! Balook'll never—"

"It's the only way!" she cried. "I don't like it myself! The Project has already paid a five thousand dollar toll—"

"Five thousand dollars!" he exclaimed, outraged anew.

"Because they'll have to close it to all traffic for at

least an hour. Duke says it was either that or a suspension bridge—''

Thor was appalled. ''Balook would jump off a bridge!''

''That's right.''

''We'd have been better off with a random route!'' Thor exclaimed. ''Balook picked his own route, coming over, and it had no problems.''

''He was lucky. What did he eat?''

''He *didn't* eat. He—'' Thor realized what he was saying. ''That's right—it'd never do this time. Still, they could've avoided the city!''

''They *should* have,'' she agreed. ''But it's too late to change it now. We're stuck with it. That's the price we pay for paying more attention to the rhinos than to the Project people.''

''And I thought this trip was going to be *fun*!'' Thor said, shaking his head glumly. Too late he realized the folly of leaving all the details to others who did not relate as closely as he to the foibles of the rhinos. He should have assumed far more responsibility. Actually, it had not only been the rhinos that had taken his attention; it had been Barb.

Responsibility: that was an adult quality. In certain ways the Project had been like a parent to him, automatically taking care of his needs as well as those of the rhinos and freak animals. He had grown dependent on that. It was time he grew up and made decisions for himself.

The freak zoo—that gave him a notion that—

''Why, am I such bad company?''

''Hey, I didn't mean—'' Then he saw her smiling,

and realized that she was teasing him. He had exclaimed about the developing horrors of this trek, and she was pretending that it was her he objected to. Well, he could fix that. "Look, I didn't hold you to that swim in the lake. I could change my mind, you know."

She assumed a look of sheer terror. "No, don't do that! Please don't do that!"

"You think only women can change their minds?" he inquired evilly.

She glanced sidelong at him. "Is there dirt on your fur?"

Thor opened his mouth, but his reply was lost in a logjam in his brain. *Had* she been talking to him in the night? Or had she realized his confusion, and now was rubbing it in?

She laughed. "I think I won that one."

"I think I'm overmatched. But it won't be funny if we have trouble in this trek."

"Most of it's okay," she said. "Just a few bad hurdles."

Thor didn't answer. He was thinking of that tunnel, and the center of town. Of the gawking spectators, and Balook's nervousness around people. And he was trying to remember the intriguing thought he had had about the freak zoo. There was something about it that might solve a significant problem—but the distraction had caused him to lose the thread.

WELCOME TO EAGLE STREAM the sign said.

It wasn't a town. It was a city. Now it was clear why the yellow line followed so many kilometers of highway: the entire neighborhood was so developed that there was no other safe route through. Decentralization had spread the population more evenly, but some industrial centers remained, and this was one of them.

All vehicles and pedestrians had been cleared from the roadbed, but in this case it was impossible to exclude the curious citizens from the region. At the fringe of that right-of-way they pressed in by the thousands. Bicycles, rickshaws, adult tricycles and electric cars jammed the accesses. Blimps and sailcraft hovered above. Balook grew increasingly nervous as the kilometers passed, and more irritable. Any little thing could set him off. Thor could tell by Theria's reactions and the tight lips of her rider that she was little better off. Only Blooky enjoyed himself; to him the massed faces were curiosities.

Another problem developed: the hot, hard pavement was uncomfortable for the rhinos' feet, which were made for treading the variable forest floor. Short stretches of concrete were all right, but this was a long stretch. The *Baluchitheria* were generally of amiable disposition, but every kilometer on this hard, hot highway eroded that.

If only there were some way to get them *off* this concourse, to take a break. But the throngs of gawking people filled every exit—and in any event, there were only more roads and houses to the sides. A city was such an awful place!

At last they came to the tunnel. Balook was so eager to get away from the sea of faces and hot pavement that he hurried into the shaded aperture without hesitation. To him it was a cave, a refuge. Where Balook led, Theria and Blooky followed.

Then some idiot turned on the tunnel lights. Balook halted so suddenly that Thor almost slid off his shoulder, and Theria nearly collided from behind. "Douse the lights!" Thor cried. "They want the shade!"

Barb got on her radio. Thor, thoughtlessly, had left his in his pack, where he could not immediately reach it. Another lesson in foresight! "Will you ask them to turn off the tunnel lights, please?" she said dulcetly, though her face was set in something very like a snarl. Thor would have admired that, if he had not been so concerned about Balook's reactions. "Yes, the rhinos can see very well in the darkness. They like the night. There will be no trouble. Please turn off the lights." She was almost grinding her teeth.

She got through. The lights went out. Balook relaxed, and so did Thor. "Thanks, Barb," he called.

"The morons!" she muttered angrily. "Those lights were supposed to stay off."

They proceeded forward in the darkness. The half-oval of the tunnel entrance receded behind. This was a big tunnel, built to accommodate the largest rigs. The ceiling was ten meters above the street surface: ample even for Balook, whose head was normally carried at an elevation of six and a half meters when he wasn't reaching up for leaves. Thor had feared the animals would suffer claustrophobia, but it was possible for them to walk abreast. Thor was vastly relieved; instead of being a hazard, the tunnel was a respite. Perhaps the rhinos thought of it as a kind of nocturnal forest, with continuous tree trunks at the sides and overhanging branches.

But they could not tarry within it. The toll covered

Eagle Stream

an hour, but that included the time it had taken to clear the traffic and the time it would take to restore it. To be sure that the total interruption fell within that limit, they had to pass through in fifteen minutes or less. That was no problem, as the distance was only two kilometers, but it left little time to dawdle. The light of the far end showed as the light of the near end faded; they were passing the slight curve at the middle.

Now Thor discovered that someone had thoughtfully put a mat of synthetic turf on the roadbed. Probably its real purpose was to protect the surface from the strike of the huge rhinos' hooves, but it also gave relief for their feet. If only they could have that on the road outside the tunnel!

Emergence was a shock. The sunlight was brilliant, and there was the noise of concentrated traffic on adjacent streets. The crowd was horrendous; it seemed as though the entire city had turned out to witness the show. They were treating it like a parade, cheering and pointing and jostling each other. Police kept order, but Thor could hardly blame Balook for disliking it. Thor could almost feel his own feet heating on the pavement, and his own sensitive ears affronted by all the noise. His own temper fraying. "Easy, Balook, easy," he repeated, over and over. "We are headed out of town, back to the forest. Just keep steady, keep walking. Ignore the freak zoo out there." Balook seemed to understand.

Then it happened. They wcrc approaching a major intersection, and though it was cordoned off, cars were moving just beyond the ropes. The moment the animals passed, this crossing would be opened for traffic again, so that the vehicles could feed into the tunnel.

A boy ducked under the rope and ran out into the street. He threw something. The object landed just behind Balook and exploded loudly.

It was a firecracker.

Balook, already near the breaking point, jumped. His head swung around, and his body jerked so violently that Thor was almost dislodged. Thor knew why: *Balook thought it was a gunshot.*

Blooky also spooked; the noise had occurred closest to him. He broke away from Theria and ran toward the boy, not realizing that the child had been the real cause of the bang. The boy scooted to the side, laughing so hard he could hardly stand up. Now there was a murmur of laughter in the crowd, too. They thought it was funny to tease the huge animals.

"Easy, Balook!" Thor cried. The rhino heard him, trusted him, and settled down. Thor knew it was largely because of confusion; Balook didn't know what to do, so he accepted the only guidance offered. Thor saw that Barb had had the presence of mind to clap her hands over Theria's ears, perhaps muffling the sound of the firecracker, and certainly making it harder for the rhino to orient for action.

But Blooky was still running, bleating piteously while the mirth of the crowd increased. The firecracker boy capered beside him, playing up to the audience. "Stop it!" Thor cried. But they ignored him, intent on their cruel fun, and he dared not dismount from Balook. The big rhino was barely under control as it was.

Blooky, terrified, careened into the barrier-rope. He now weighed a hundred and fifty kilograms. The rope

A boy ducked under the rope

spanged, and several people leaning on it tumbled to the ground. One young woman landed with her skirt whipped up over her head, to the delight of nearby voyeurs. The cries of surprise, glee and dismay alarmed Blooky further. He bounced off the rope and staggered on toward the intersection. Then he saw an opening in the crowd, leaped over the rope, and ran into the traffic beyond.

"No, Blooky!" Thor and Barb screamed together. But the animal kept going, blindly. He ran out in front of a slowly moving car. The car struck him, knocking him down. He gave a bleat of anguish.

Balook obviously had not seen precisely what had happened; his daytime sight was not sharp. But Blooky's cry electrified him. Thor's alarm flared too; he had noted the way Balook regarded any potential threat to his offspring. Balook normally did not seem to pay Blooky much attention, reacting mainly to Theria's signals. But now every muscle in Balook's back went taut. Theria, oddly, seemed more relaxed; perhaps she was deferring to Balook on this matter. Violence was mostly male business.

"No, Balook!" Thor cried—with no more effect than before. Balook lurched into motion, enraged. He charged the car.

The firecracker boy was still dancing about, reveling in the attention of the crowd. Balook's lifting forefoot struck him, hurling him aside like a plastic doll. Then the rope snapped as the rhino plowed through it. All Thor could do was hang on, knowing he was amidst ongoing disaster; he had lost any semblance of control.

The car that had hit Blooky had stopped. Balook

reared like a stallion. Thor grabbed a double handful of skin and fur and hung on desperately, nine meters high as the massive shoulders lifted. His feet dangled. The supply pack swung around. Then the expansion of Balook's muscles snapped the pack's strap, and it dropped to the street. Thor didn't dare try to grab for it; he had to maintain his hold, lest he fall too. He could be crushed if he fell.

The rhino's two forefeet came down on the roof of the car. The metal crumpled like tin foil, and from inside came an awful scream and crackle of shorted electricity.

Now the police had appeared, and they were drawing guns. That was all that was needed to complete the disaster! The moment a gun fired, Balook would go berserk, striking at anything that moved. Thor knew it, and knew he could do nothing to stop it.

Except—to get Balook out of here! It was the rhino's natural instinct to stampede when alarmed. If he could just start Balook going—

"Run, Balook, run!" Thor cried, kicking the huge shoulders. How often they had played this game as youngsters, he and the rhino. Charging about the Project . . .

It worked! Balook, seeing the open road ahead, ran. The pavement shook under the impact of his mighty feet, and small cracks radiated. People scrambled out of the way, and cars screeched to the side to make a clear passage. Balook was larger than he had been, and more powerful, and more agressive, and he moved faster: a good fifty kilometers per hour in the charge. Thor hung on.

At least he was getting Balook out of immediate danger. Already the houses were thinning, and the open countryside was manifesting. Balook had forgotten Theria and Blooky for the moment; that was the limited advantage of limited intelligence. By the time he remembered, he would be safe, and Barb would be seeing to the other two.

But how would the five of them get back together again, and back on the yellow trail? Thor had done what was necessary, what was expedient at the moment, to prevent Balook from doing any more carnage in the city. But already he was sick at the thought of the consequence of what had already happened.

BALOOK COULD RUN, and swiftly, but not forever. Gradually he slowed. By this time the city was behind, and the countryside was back: fields, farm, and islands of trees. Thor relaxed, no longer in danger of being shaken loose.

But now that he was able to think, Thor found little comfort. People had been hurt or killed—he wasn't sure which—and that could mean that Balook's life was forfeit. They could cut cross-country to intersect the yellow line and in due course reconnect with Barb and Theria and Blooky—but what use would that be now? The authorities would set up a posse and come after Balook, and that would be that. Outside folk wouldn't care that Balook was special, or that he had not been at fault; he was an animal, and therefore had few if any rights.

He brooded on that. Why *didn't* animals have rights? Was the human species so selfish that it could afford to consider no welfare but its own?

Thor had no radio; that had been in the pack. He could not call Barb to learn the worst. Was Theria all right? Had Blooky survived? He had seen Blooky struck, seen him fall, but the car had been moving slowly; it should not be serious. But how could he be sure? There was no way to find out except to go back—and he couldn't do that until he knew the nature of the charges against Balook. He was not going to deliver Balook into execution, or even into doubt!

So they walked on, staying off the road and away from farmsteads. Thor was hungry, but food was secondary. How could he save Balook from whatever threatened him?

By hiding him, he realized. But how could he hide a creature whose head rose seven or eight meters above the ground? Balook was as tall as small trees; he had to be, to graze on them! But he did not look remotely like a tree! How, then, could he be hidden among trees?

Thor considered, and decided that it was possible. After all, deer and other wild animals hid pretty successfully in the forest. The trick was to leave little or no trail, and to be where the pursuers were not. One tree could not hide a huge animal, several trees could not, but a forest full of trees could.

"Let's go another way, Balook," he said, kicking gently on the side from which he wanted to turn. Balook obeyed. Thor guided him along the hardest ground he could spy, so that he left few clear prints. Dogs could sniff them out, and probably experienced woodsmen could follow the spoor, but the average posse would perhaps soon lose it. That was the best he could do.

They approached a power line. Tall metal towers extended in a straight line across the landscape. Was this part of the same corridor he had seen two years before, when searching for Balook? Possibly; those lines extended all over the continent, and were interconnected, so they could be considered all parts of the same monstrous system. The giant rhino of wires, the biggest of the big! The corridor was fenced off, but Balook merely stepped over the two-meter fence and proceeded to munch the foliage within at the six and seven meter elevation. For the moment he seemed to be satisfied to remain away from Theria and Blooky, but Thor was not sure how long that would last.

He crawled down Balook's sloping back, slid along the broad rump, and caught hold of the tail. He handed himself on down, using the tail like a rope. Balook was of course used to this, and tolerated it; it would have been a different matter with a stranger. The tail's tassel hung about two meters above the ground, which made it quite handy as a ladder.

They were safe, for a while. There had been no evidence of pursuit, and much of the ground had been hard enough to make Thor's effort of obscuration successful. Who would suspect Balook of hiding in the corridor of a power line? In fact it offered fair concealment, because the high wires would screen the view somewhat from above.

Balook seemed calm now. If he missed his mate and calf, there was still no evidence of it. That seemed to be a difference between the animal nature and human nature: the human worried about his absent friends and relatives. There was no doubt that Balook *cared*, as his attack on the car that hit Blooky had shown, but he simply did not concern himself about absent rhinos. Unless they happened to be in heat, so that the smell alerted him. Awareness was immediate. Probably the animal lacked the ability to visualize distant things, or to make theoretical constructions.

Could that account for *Baluchitherium*'s extinction? If family members got separated from each other, and saber-toothed tigers attacked one while the other was peacefully grazing elsewhere . . . or if a baby fell in a hole and disappeared, and the mother didn't hear, so had no concern. A fatal flaw in the species, perhaps.

Thor shook his head. He was no paleontological scholar; probably the reason the species died out was something comparatively mundane, like insufficient foraging room when the climate changed. If there were a blight on suitable trees, the species would be in trouble in a hurry, because of its huge feeding demands. It was dangerous to make assumptions based on comparisons with human beings, whose lifestyle was quite different. Few animals needed the ability to theorize!

But right now, Thor almost wished the human mind were the same. Then he would not be bothered by phantoms. If anything had happened to Barb . . .

He found a stream crossing the power line aisle, about a kilometer along. He flung himself down and drank deeply. Water had never tasted so good!

Balook heard him and moved to the stream. When *he* drank, the river threatened to dry up!

There were a few wild berries growing beside the fence. Thor walked along, picking the ripe blackberries and popping them into his mouth. It was a slow way to get a meal, but it was sure. When he came to a particularly plentiful patch, he sat down and cleaned it out. He realized that he would have been out of luck in winter, while Balook—well, the big rhino preferred deciduous foliage, but could handle pine needles, and of course much of his sustenance was derived from the twigs and branches and bark. So yes, Balook could survive in winter, in the wild. If left alone.

Thor heard something. It was now midafternoon, and he happened to be sitting in shadow. Balook was on down the line, out of sight for the moment. Thor froze, listening and watching. Something was coming through the field beyond the trees bordering the power line corridor.

It was a man—and he carried a rifle.

Suddenly Thor's heart was pounding. Nobody carried a rifle or any gun openly, unless authorized—and only the police and military personnel were authorized. There was only one good reason the police would be walking out here.

They were after Balook!

It had been sheer luck that Balook had run so far along the highway before diverging into the fields and forest, because no footprints showed there. Thor had done his best to eliminate traces, once he realized the danger they represented. So the police didn't know exactly where to start looking, and were combing the area. This was slow and wasteful and probably spread thin—but before long they would surely discover the few tracks Balook had left, and then they would orient and close in on the rhino himself. That would be the end.

It was a man—and he carried a rifle

Thor waited until the rifleman dropped out of sight in a gully. Then he ran for cover behind the power line brush. It was like a thin strip of forest between the fences; rabbits scooted out of sight as Thor ran, and birds fluttered in the line of trees. But it was too thin to hide Balook, especially considering the noise the rhino made, tearing branches off high trunks and crunching them up. Even the rhino's tumultuous noises of digestion could be heard at some distance, and when he broke wind the sound could carry distressingly far.

Breathless, Thor ran up to Balook. "Trouble!" he gasped. "We've got to get out of here!"

Balook cocked his head, dangling a mouthful of brush. Leaves, twigs, wood, bark—here was the proof that it was all much the same to this monster appetite! But it had to be stifled now. "Balook, this is a matter of life and death. *Your* life and death! We've got to move out in a hurry!"

Balook, of course, could not understand the words. But he caught the urgency of the tone, and lowered his head so that Thor could mount. Thor scrambled over the mouthful of brush, for the rhino, like other animals, was unable to conduct two conscious operations simultaneously, and chewing stopped when attention was distracted. They stepped over the fence opposite the side the rifleman was approaching, and moved out at cruising speed. Thor hoped they would get away unnoticed.

If they were spotted, Balook could probably outrun the police vehicles, because he could maintain velocity cross-country while they would be confined largely to roads. Unless there was a copter—but copters were scarce, and it normally took days to requisition one.

A car shot across the field ahead. "Oh, no!" Thor groaned. "That's a floater!"

The floaters traveled on a cushion of air. They floated over the terrain at respectable velocity, requiring no pavement. Rocks and ridges hardly affected them, and they could traverse level water too.

Thor pondered feverishly. How could they avoid this pursuit? The floater's main weakness was thick forest, because it required space to pass between the trees; close-set saplings could balk it. But here there was no suitable forest. Another problem was hilly country. The floater lost power when too steeply tilted, because the air cushion depended on proper balance. But there were no mountains in the immediate vicinity, or even any good hills. Still, if they could lead it through a gully—

"Head for the stream, Balook!" Thor cried. But it was the pressure of his knees, not his words, that made the command clear. Balook swerved, and soon was tramping down toward the little stream they had drunk from.

The car followed. There was no doubt it was after them; it reoriented unerringly when their route changed. It did not enter the gully, but moved along the edge. Its driver knew better than to charge that steep incline. Too bad.

Thor saw something glint from the car window. A gun! They could shoot Balook down from a distance! The gully was too small to get the rhino out of range; the car would keep following the rim.

They had to put the car out of commission. Thor knew only one way. A floater could not function when tilted—or turned over. Like a turtle, it was helpless on its back.

If Balook could kick it over . . .

But someone might be hurt in the car, or even killed. Could he afford to risk that?

He saw the glint of the gun again. It was taking aim! If he didn't stop it, *Balook* could be killed!

"Charge!" he yelled, urging Balook up the slope, directly toward the car.

This was another game Balook understood. He turned and charged. Stones and dirt spewed out of the bank as his giant hooves pounded through.

There was a shot. Balook jumped, and Thor knew the animal had been hit. But no ordinary bullet could bring down a creature this size. "Keep going, Balook! Knock that car over!"

Balook closed on the car. Now the vehicle dodged, trying to avoid him—and too late Thor realized his mistake. Balook's freshest memory of cars was the one that had struck Blooky. Now a car was attacking Balook himself; he had had experience with firearms, and knew the significance of the noise from the car and the strike of the bullet. There was murder in the rhino's pain-tormented mind.

Balook reared, lifting his forefeet. "No!" Thor cried, knowing that what happened would be his fault.

But the car zipped aside, and the terrible hooves missed. The ground shook, and a fallen branch sailed into the air, levered up by the force of the strike. Balook's great mass made his attack slow, and the driver knew how to maneuver.

There were no more shots. Evidently there was only

one man in the car, and he had to concentrate on his driving now, and could not get oriented for another attack. But the moment Balook let the car go, that gun would speak again.

How could they get out of this? They could afford neither to smash the car nor to flee it.

Balook, maddened by pain and memory, had his own notion. He reared again—and again the car dodged out of the way. This time a hoof caught part of a fallen, rotten trunk, and there was a spray of water and vapor. Balook had power, yes—but that approach was hopeless. The rhino could not catch the vehicle.

"Your nose, Balook!" Thor cried. "Lift it over!" But again his words were useless. How could he make the rhino understand? Balook's neck was so strong he could readily overturn the car, and it would be an unexpected move that might work.

But Balook was unable either to understand or to reason it out for himself. The survival of his species had been based on size, not intelligence. He reared again—and again the car dodged.

The wrong way. It dropped into the gully, tilted, and lost power. By accident Balook had done the right thing! He had disabled the car without touching it.

"Run!" Thor cried, and now Balook ran. This command was in his repertoire. He had seen the car fall and die; vengeance had been achieved. Soon they left the police behind.

Thor guided Balook along a road, so as to hide his hoofprints. But there were two things wrong with this strategy. There was traffic on this road, both pedal and electric, making concealment impossible—and Balook was bleeding from the gunshot wound. Huge drops of bright red blood splattered on the pavement, leaving an obvious trail.

So it had to be cross-country again—and how were they to escape? It was now late afternoon; if they could avoid direct pursuit until dark, maybe . . .

But Balook slowed, limping. The wound had seemed minor in the throes of battle with the floater, but now that excitement was over, and much blood was being lost.

They stopped in a patch of forest, and Thor looked at the wound. It was in Balook's huge belly. Blood streamed from it. A man would have been dead already, but Balook's mass was so much greater that it was less serious for him. Obviously it had been no BB gun in that car; more like an elephant gun.

"God, Balook, that's bad!" Thor exclaimed, appalled. "There's no telling how much damage it's done inside. We've got to stop the blood!"

He ripped a handful of leaves from a bush and approached Balook. But the injury was well out of his reach. Balook could lie down, but Thor didn't want to ask him to do that. For one thing, it might aggravate the wound; for another, it would interfere with the animal's eating. After the long trek and run, Balook should be ravenous.

Assuming that the wound had not messed up his gut and his digestion. If that was the case—

Thor shook off the grim thought. He found a rock and several pieces of fallen wood. He piled them up, so that he could stand half a meter higher. This brought him just within range. He mopped at the wound.

The leaves came away caked with blood. A huge partial clot fell into his hand, and the bleeding increased.

Horrified, Thor stared at the red mass. "I'm making it worse!" he said. He had seen blood before, but never in this quantity. He felt nauseated and dizzy. This was Balook's life that was pouring out!

Thor steeled himself. This was no time for faintheartedness! He had to keep his wits about him, so that he could help Balook.

First, he had to stop meddling with the wound. There was no way he could bandage it, and it might succeed in clotting itself closed if he just let it alone. Second, he had to think this thing through and decide on a course of action.

Item: Balook was eating well. That meant that the intestinal system had not been badly damaged; his fear about that had been premature. Balook also moved readily, so the muscles were all right.

Item: there was no hole opposite the wound, so the bullet had not passed all the way through Balook's body. The metal was lodged somewhere inside. That wasn't good, but it might after all be that the bullet was small, and had made a much larger and more ragged puncture because it was moving slowly. Balook was so massive that penetration might have been slight, relatively. So maybe this amounted to a flesh wound: painful, gory, but not serious.

Thor felt better. Now he had things in better proportion. Balook could lose several liters of blood, and it would be no worse than a few grams for a man. No immediate worry.

But suppose there were infection, or metal poisoning, from the embedded bullet?

Thor struggled with the notion for a moment, then dismissed it. There was nothing he could do except hope.

As night came, Thor mounted Balook again and hung on, so that he would not become separated from the animal. Balook might feed the better part of the night, and this was good, because he needed plenty of nutrition to make up for the loss of blood and to restore his vitality. But he might move several kilometers in the course of his browsing, and the police could catch up at any time. Thor had to be with him when that happened, for Thor now represented Balook's intelligence. Thor might know what to do in an emergency when Balook didn't.

So he laid his head against Balook's flexing neck, and hooked both hands into the loose skin of the shoulders. He could sleep this way, so long as Balook moved slowly. He had done it before, years ago, when Balook had been lonely. Balook himself would take care that he didn't shake Thor loose.

He nodded off, his left ear against the base of Balook's great neck. In this position he could hear the sounds of the animal's feeding: the crunching of the huge teeth transmitted along the bones of the column of the neck, the big masses of masticated foliage being swallowed, the more distant rumblings and gurglings of the digestive process. It was a comforting cacophony; it meant that all systems were functioning.

Thor dreamed of Barbara Hartford. Only she wasn't called that any more. She was Barbara Hartford Nem-

"C'mon, let's swim!"

men, in a lovely bridal gown, smiling, saying "C'mon, let's swim!"

He woke, shaking with the realization: he loved her. He wanted to marry her. Perhaps he always had, since their first meeting, when he had seen how well she understood about Balook. He just hadn't been able to admit it, so had cut himself off from her as well as from Balook. He found it hard, now, to imagine how he could have been guilty of such colossal folly.

But as his head cleared, the passion faded. They were too young, really, to marry—and Barb had shown no such inclination. She worked with him because she had to, to get the rhinos moved to the Eastern Project site. She was civil because it was better than being bitter. But love? Why should he fool himself!

He wished there were some way to make it up to her, so that they could start again, all-the-way fresh, so that romance would be possible instead of mere friendship. Then, abruptly, his lost notion of the prior night returned. The freak zoo—

Balook stumbled. Alarmed, Thor called out. "Hey, Balook—you okay?" It was still dark, so Thor couldn't see the wound. But now he realized that the animal had stopped eating, and was moving slowly. The skin of the neck felt hot against Thor's face.

He lifted his head, alarmed. The infection, the loss of blood—they had gotten to Balook!

No, maybe the rhino was just tired, ready to lie down and sleep. Of course his body was hot; it was always hot in late day and early evening, because of his mechanism of temperature modulation. It was practically impossible to tell when he was running an abnormal fever, because he so often ran normal fevers. Still, an infection-fever could not be ruled out. It might not be detectable at skin-surface, but could be ravaging the vital inner organs.

Balook often slept standing, but this time it might be better lying down. "Sure, Balook; I'll get off!"

He scrambled along the back and slid down the tail and stood aside. Balook kneeled, then lay. That was all, thank God!

Thor walked around to Balook's head, patted his nose, and leaned against the big jaw. He settled down, braced against the monstrous head, one arm half encircling an ear, providing what comfort he could. In that position they slept the rest of the night.

THE MORNING WAS pleasant, but what it revealed was not. A silent blimp was hovering hardly two kilometers away, and there could be no doubt about its mission. Thor stood at the edge of the forest and watched it slowly move back and forth.

The police had to know Balook was in here, and the blimp was there to make sure he could not escape unobserved. Since fields surrounded these trees, that ploy would work. The patch of forest was smaller than he had supposed yesterday evening; its broadest width was no more than a kilometer.

Thor went back to inspect Balook—and found to his dismay that the rhino had not yet gotten to his feet.

"Balook, are you all right?" Stupid question; a better one would be "How bad is it?"

At Thor's urging, Balook struggled to raise himself, sank down again, lifted, and finally made it to his feet.

The wound came into sight. It seemed to have scabbed over somewhat; there was some oozing from it, but the flow of blood had stopped.

Yet Balook was staggering like a newborn calf, hardly able to keep his balance. Thor stepped back, afraid the rhino would accidentally step on him. What was wrong?

He knew what was wrong, when he unblocked his resistive mind. Infection!

No—if that were the case, Balook should have a raging fever, and he didn't. Thor had slept against him all night, and verified that in the morning the fur was warm only where Thor's own body had rested against it. If there was any fever, it was slight. Balook had cooled overnight in his normal fashion.

Then what? With no fever, and no more bleeding, and several hours' rest—

Bleeding? Thor struck the heel of his hand against his forehead. This too he had thought of before, and too eagerly dismissed. There *was* bleeding—but not where it showed! Balook could be hemorrhaging internally, filling his bowel with blood, liters of it! Now he was out on his feet, weak from that tremendous night's loss. A loss that might still be occurring.

Then Thor heard something ominous. It was the baying of a dog.

The police were on the trail now, and in minutes they would be here. This time there would be no escape, for Balook was too weak to run.

And even if he *could* run, and got away—how could Balook survive? Thor was no doctor; he could not do

Balook had heard the dog too

a thing about the hemorrhaging. Balook would die anyway. There was no way out.

Balook had heard the dog too. Now that sound was augmented by human voices, and several motors. All getting louder.

Balook tried to run. ''Wait for me!'' Thor cried, lifting his arms. Balook halted, swinging his head down toward him—and lost his balance.

Down he came, falling as only twelve tons could fall. Thor barely jumped clear in time to avoid being crushed by the tremendous body. But his horror was for the damage he knew that fall was doing to Balook's internal organs. Even an elephant could be killed by a fall of only one or two meters, and Balook was twice that size. His guts could burst.

Thor looked at the fallen giant, appalled. Balook moved his head weakly. He was in pain, now; perhaps he had been in pain all along, but not shown it. That pain had now progressed too far to be ignored—and there was nothing Thor could do.

How could all this have come about, because of one brat with a firecracker? Mixed with Thor's grief for Balook was sheer, blinding rage at that capering boy. At that moment he hoped the boy was dead.

There was the crashing of brush as men tramped through the forest, closing in. It had not been much of a chase, after all, and there had been only one possible outcome. Balook would die—whether captive or free.

Suddenly Thor's rage overcame him. They had no right to do this! Balook was innocent; he should not suffer for what heartless ignorant people had done!

The men were coming with guns. He could tell where they were by the clumsy sounds, though they did not yet see him or Balook. Thor could overcome one of them, get his gun, drive them off . . .

"I'll take care of you, Balook!" he said. "Trust me!"

Balook's head dropped slowly to the ground, reassured. Despite the disparity of their sizes, Thor had always been the one to protect Balook in the human world.

Thor ran to a large tree and scrambled up it. If he were lucky, they would pass this way. Like a panther, he waited, alternately savage and afraid. If only there were some better way out—but there wasn't.

The first man came—from the wrong direction. He held a dog on a leash. Thor despaired.

"Hey, we found it!" the man cried.

"On my way!" another called. In a moment he walked directly under Thor's tree. He carried a rifle.

Thor jumped. He was no panther; his takeoff was

clumsy, and his shirt hung up on a broken limb. It ripped loudly, and he was jerked off his course. He fell behind his prey, landing heavily on the ground.

The man whirled around, rifle ready. Thor lunged at him, grabbing for the weapon. He had no balance and no plan, except to get that rifle. His hands caught hold of the barrel, and he yanked as hard as he could.

The man jerked back. Thor, offbalanced, fell—but he had it! He had the rifle! He rolled on the ground, but got his finger on the trigger. "Stop where you are!" he cried.

The two men stopped. "Why, it's just a boy!" one said.

"Get out of here!" Thor said, pointing the rifle at the nearest man. "Leave Balook alone!"

"Put it down," the man said. "The animal is dying."

There was no way to argue with that. Already other policemen were approaching.

"Will you promise to help him?" Thor pleaded. "He didn't really do anything!"

The men exchanged glances. "We can't promise," one said.

"But we'll do what we can," the other added.

What choice was there? Thor dropped the rifle and stared into the ground. Then he walked back to Balook and hugged the prostrate neck as well as he could manage. "Somehow, somehow . . ." he whispered to the nearest ear, the tears coming unashamedly.

"OH, THOR!" BARB cried. "What *happened*?"

"Balook got shot . . ." He shook his head, sickened by the whole thing. "What happened to *you*?"

They were in the forest, not far from Balook. Thor could not leave the rhino—not now. He had promised to take care of Balook, and Balook trusted him, and he had to carry through somehow. Two veterinarians were working on the wound. Balook was unconscious, under sedation. The loss of blood had put him most of the way out before the medication started.

"Blooky broke his leg, but he's all right," she said. "It was more of a bend than a break, actually. He's got a splint, and he's young enough to think it's just part of life. Theria stayed put. We're all right. But you—"

"The man in the car! Did they—?"

"He escaped with severe bruises. The driver's compartment was specially braced. Still, it was lucky Balook didn't hit it one more time!"

"The firecracker brat!" Thor demanded. "*He* started it!"

"I don't know! They took him away so soon—"

Thor didn't push it. They both knew that the boy was either dead or critically injured. Thor would have been satisfied to see the boy in hell, but then Balook would be guilty of murder. So he had to hope grudgingly that the brat survived.

"How did Balook get shot?" Barb asked anxiously. "The police were under orders to shoot only in self defense."

"We didn't know that," Thor said, horrified anew. Had he brought it on Balook by his own action? "I saw the glint from the gun, and thought they were going to shoot him right away. We charged the floater . . ." He trailed off. What was the use in talking about it?

"I've got to get back to Blooky and Theria," Barb said. "She gets nervous without me. But first I've got to know about Balook!"

They walked over to the downed animal. Open surgery was in progress. "We're fishing for the bullet," one vet told him.

"How—how bad—?" Thor asked, finding himself squeamish. It was not the sight of the blood and instruments, but that it was the body of his friend. It could as readily have been an autopsy . . .

"The intestine has been damaged, but no vital organs were hit. The main problem is loss of blood and exhaustion. Maybe some infection. If we can get the bullet out and keep him quiet, he should pull through."

"Thank God!" Barb breathed.

The vet looked at her. "You'd better hope that boy has similar luck," he said. Then he plunged his hand back into Balook's gut, searching for the bullet.

They didn't answer. There was no answer to make. They walked toward the car that was waiting for Barb.

She stopped outside it. "Thor—"

"Yes?" He was so concerned about Balook that he wasn't really paying attention.

"Thor, when I thought—that is, when you were gone, and the dragnet was after you—I didn't know whether you were alive or dead. Anything could have happened! I—"

"Balook's still in trouble," he said. "We still don't know."

"Not Balook. *You.* I mean, Balook too, of course. But—"

"I'm okay. Tired, that's all. Balook took good care of me." He tried to smile, but the humor was vacant.

"Will you shut up and *listen* a moment?" she flared.

His eyes jerked from the rhino to her. "What's the matter, Barb?"

"Can't we go somewhere and talk?"

"I can't leave Balook. Not while he's sick."

"Well, here, then. Thor, I—well, it's crazy, but I—" She stamped her foot in frustration. "Oh, I can't *say* it!"

"Barb, did I do something? I'm sorry. It's just that I'm so concerned about Balook I hardly know what else is happening."

"So am I," she said. "It's not that. I'm glad you're concerned."

There was an awkward silence. "You know, Barb," he said at last, realizing that she needed time to work out what she was going to say. ''I dreamed about you last night.''

''You did?'' she asked, taking his arm. ''What kind of dream?''

''It's foolish. Nothing to it,'' he said, embarrassed.

''So I'm nothing?'' she asked with mock ire.

''No, not that at all!''

''What, then? C'mon, tell me.'' She smiled, mocking herself.

''I'd rather not say. You'd laugh—or be mad.''

''No I wouldn't. Tell me.''

He met her gaze. Her face was beautiful, as lovely as his dream. He threw caution to the wind. ''That we were—man and wife. Or about to be. At least, you were in a bridal gown. And you said 'C'mon, let's swim!' ''

She remained silent. Her expression did not change.

He felt the flush rising. ''I warned you it was foolish,'' he said defensively. ''Just a crazy dream. I shouldn't have told you.''

''Yes, it's foolish,'' she agreed. ''We're too young, we have so much to learn, so much growing to do. But sort of sweet. Did you really dream that, or did you make it up?''

''I really did dream it.'' He had not yet fathomed her reaction. Was she amused—or not amused? ''It—it's pretty transparent wish-fulfillment, I guess. That swim—it's all tied up with—I wish I'd—I don't know.'' He wished he had never opened his mouth!

''Me too,'' she murmured.

His head whipped around. ''What?''

"That's what I was trying to tell you. I dreamed we were at the lake and—swimming."

"That's not the same." But his heart was beating.

"To me it is." She glanced sidelong at him. "And to you too, I think."

"I guess so." His chagrin was converting to relief and even to joy. "I just didn't want you to think that I just wanted to see you—you know."

"I do know, Thor. I feel the same. The symbolism is obvious. To see each other without shame—the way married people do. We already know how similar we are, the good and the bad."

"We have to keep it in perspective," he said, addressing himself as much as her. He felt as if he were sailing over a river on the bike, aware how quickly and devastatingly he could flip out of control if he lost his balance. "It's a time of stress, of crisis. Maybe we're just reacting to that."

"We probably are," she agreed. "No sense getting carried away and maybe making a bad mistake."

"No sense at all," he said, longing for her. But then he looked at Balook, and knew that *nothing* made any sense while the rhino's fate was in doubt.

"C'mon, kiss me," Barb said.

Was it another dream? Thor set that question aside and seized the moment. He kissed her, not hard.

For a moment it was strange, a repeat of the first kiss, and he feared she would push him away again, that she had been joking, that he had missed the point and ruined it by his eagerness. But then her arms came up to wrap around his neck, to draw him in closer, and it was like orbiting in space, disembodied except for that miraculous contact of their lips and the clasp of her arms.

At last they broke. The entire forest seemed brighter, richer, like the beauty of dusk when colors were enhanced. Barb was so lovely it was almost painful to look at her.

"I won't say I love you," she said. "But I guess I don't have to."

"I think you just did," he remarked wryly. "Barb—can't you bring Theria and Blooky out here? So we can all be together? I can't leave him, and I don't want to leave you."

"I'll try," she promised.

"Damn it, I *will* say it!" he exclaimed. "I *do*—"

She jumped to put her hand over his mouth. "No—no! We can't say anything we might regret."

"I'll never regret it!"

She quirked a smile. "Have you never done something you regretted?"

"For two years!" Which brought home to him the validity of her caution.

"Wait until we know about Balook."

She was right. He nodded. "Come if you can," he said, turning away. He did not dare remain with her longer, lest he make a scene that would embarrass them both.

He heard the car door close. Then the car hummed slowly along the path cleared for vehicles, headed for the nearest road. Thor turned to wave, then walked on toward Balook.

Then he remembered that notion about the freak zoo. They had been operating under the assumption that

"I won't say I love you."

they would separate after the rhinos were delivered to the Eastern Project site, and that there would no longer be a job for her. But the zoo needed people who related well to strange animals, and if Barb—

"Got it!" one vet cried, holding up a bloody something. "Bullet's out. I believe he'll pull through, with proper care."

"I'll stay with him!" Thor said.

"He'll need more than that," the man said. "We'll have to put him on special feed, and he'll need a lot of it. Nourishment that won't aggravate the intestine. And he'll have to be kept warm."

"But Balook doesn't have any trouble with the chill of the night," Thor protested. "He has his own ways to handle both heat and cold."

The man glanced at him. "Such as?"

"He allows the excess heat to accumulate in the outer layers by day, then draws on it at night. His body temperature varies far more widely than ours does. His mass is so great that it changes slowly anyway."

"And how does he build up this heat?"

"Why, mostly from exercise—" Thor broke off, finally getting the vet's point. Balook was sick, and could not move about and forage while he recovered from the injury. He would slowly cool off, and not be able to recharge his heat in his normal manner. "Maybe blankets—"

The man shook his head. "Never work. Animals don't understand blankets. We'll have to put up a tent."

Thor realized that this was going to be expensive. "I don't know if we can get a requisition in time."

"You had better call your Project Manager and impress upon him the need," the vet warned.

"That's not the problem. He will know the need. It's that it takes days to requisition anything out of the ordinary. The bureaucracy just doesn't move any faster."

The man considered. "There may be another way. I'll ask the Mayor."

"Mayor?" Thor asked blankly.

"Mayor Caldwell of Eagle Stream."

"You mean the town we just—?"

"I'll handle it," the man said. He went to his truck and began talking on the radio.

Soon he was back. "A tent's on the way, along with the other equipment and supplies we need. Be here in an hour."

"But how—?"

"The Mayor's coming out with the first load. He'll talk to you."

"To me?" Thor was baffled by this development.

"He'll update you. He's good at that."

Thor did not pursue the subject. He could think of no optimistic reason why such a personage should make a personal call. Was the city going to sue the Project—or merely jail Thor and Barb on suspicion of homicide?

Balook was sleeping. Thor realized that it must have taken a lot of sedation to put twelve tons to sleep, and it would take time to wear off. But the first crisis was past; the vet said the rhino would make it.

All too soon the Mayor arrived. He was an old man, but still spry. He reminded Thor somewhat of his grandfather; he had the same gray mane, and similar lines about the face.

"Thor Nemmen?" Mayor Caldwell inquired heartily, shaking hands. "Don't worry about a thing. We have the report on what happened; your animals were not at fault. Eagle Stream will take care of you."

Already the tent was going up: an inflated-wall type of considerable size. It wouldn't fit in the forest, so they were pitching it in the field.

"Thank you, sir," Thor said, looking for the catch. "But this must be very expensive—"

"Yes, and we shall take care of that, too," the Mayor said. "The people want to see your animals. We'll rope off the area and charge admission—"

"Charge admission!" Thor cried, shocked.

"Now don't misunderstand, son. We're sorry about what happened, and we feel responsible. That boy should never have gotten into your right of way. But I would soon be out of office if I didn't protect the taxpayer's interest. We'll control entry, and post warnings; troublemakers won't get near your animal."

"Balook's no freak!"

"Of course not, son, of course not. But he *is* impressive. Long time since the citizens of Eagle Stream have seen a horse that size."

"He's a rhino, not a horse!"

"Of course. We'll explain that the fee goes directly to the support of the animal. That way, the town can make it up to you."

"This is ridiculous! Balook doesn't like crowds!"

"Son, you've got to understand. The citizens are sorry, and they want to help. My phone's been busy all morning. Give them a chance to salve their consciences. Your animal will like them, when he sees how decent they are."

The prospect appalled Thor, but beneath the Mayor's homey manner there was a genuine financial imperative. Balook did need help, and needed it now, not days from now when the Project authorization came through. The Project personnel had not even been able to get here yet; they were evidently helpless.

"Could you bring the others here—Theria and Blooky?" Thor asked.

"We intend to. Is the calf amenable to petting? That would be a great attraction for the children."

"Look, Mayor Caldwell—if someone hurts Blooky, the same thing will happen all over again!"

The Mayor looked Thor in the eye. He had a remarkably level gaze. "Son, trust me. No one will hurt any of your animals. There will be no trouble. I know how to organize these things. Just sign this release—"

"I already saw how you organize things! That's why Balook's hurt!"

"I see we have a slight misunderstanding," the Mayor said. "Several, in fact. First, I did not organize your journey through Eagle City; I was against it, for reasons that are obvious now. But I was overruled by the City Council, some of whose members may discover themselves seeking new employment before long. Second, you need the help I'm offering; your animal will surely die if left untended, and your Project is unable to make the necessary arrangements quickly enough. Third, you lack legal status; your animal is trespassing on private property. Fourth, there are certain criminal charges—"

"I'll sign the paper," Thor said. He wasn't certain how binding his signature would be, because he was only Balook's guide, technically, as well as being underage, but he had lost his taste for quibbling. The Mayor had evidently thought things out better than Thor had.

"A very reasonable attitude," the Mayor said, presenting him with a pen.

AS IT TURNED out, the Mayor was right and Thor's worries wrong. The cordon about the area prevented random intrusions, and unarmed police kept the sightseers subdued. There were many children, but they were well behaved. Hours of visitation were limited, with regular breaks for the rhinos. Barb stayed in a little pen with Blooky, who was wearing a plastic cast on his leg. The little rhino took quite a liking to the attentions of the children, who invariably brought treats. (The Treat Concession was adjacent; the city was making money there, too.) Even Theria condescended to give rides when properly bribed by flavorful leafy branches imported for the occasion, though only when Barb was aboard with the children. The animals were in danger of becoming spoiled.

Balook was left alone in his heated tent, except for the attention of the vets. In a few days he was on his feet again, supplementing the concentrated feed with selective browsing. Spectators were permitted reasonably close, and Balook became accustomed to them. Adults and children goggled at the dispatch with which the huge rhino crunched whole branches as his digestion mended.

The animals were in danger of becoming spoiled

Things were looking up. Soon Balook and Blooky would be well enough to travel again.

Then the firecracker boy died.

"They're going to put Balook on trial for manslaughter," Barb said. "You know what that means."

"It means they'll kill him," Thor said.

"Not if we put up a good enough defense!"

"You know the law," Thor said grimly. "If a man kills an animal, the man is fined or imprisoned. If an animal kills a man, the animal dies."

"But it was an accident!" she cried. "The boy was tormenting them! Everyone saw it!"

"Everyone saw Balook hit him. That's evidence enough."

"Look," she said determinedly. "Balook never saw that boy. He was running toward Blooky and the car, and the boy just got in the way. If a man drives a car too fast and hits someone in the street, it's just an accident. Manslaughter."

"Like a car . . ." Thor said, something nagging at his mind.

"Balook's *not* a car!" Barb snapped. "I just meant—"

"Oh, now I've lost it," Thor said, frustrated.

"Lost what?"

"The thought. Something about Balook."

Barb shrugged. "We'd better do more than *think* about Balook. He needs a lawyer."

"We can't hire a lawyer. Our funds have been frozen, pending the trial. Mr. Duke's been going crazy!"

"I know that!" she retorted sharply. "The State will provide one. Only—"

"That's all we need. A third-rate assignee."

"Give him a chance," she said, but her defense lacked conviction. "We don't even know who he is, yet."

"Do we need to?"

Her look was dismal. "What can we do, Thor?"

He shook his head, seeing no real solution. If the senior personnel of the Project were unable to act, how could a pair of penniless teenagers? This incident had ruined everything. "We can pray for a miracle, maybe."

"C'mon, kiss me."

"Despair makes you romantic?" he asked, dismayed.

"We're stymied with Balook. We're not stymied with each other. Let's do something about what's possible. Maybe the other will work out, somehow.''

Thor wasn't sure about the rationale, but hardly cared to argue. He kissed her, and then things did seem more optimistic.

THE LAWYER WAS Mr. Twild: small, old, bald, and he carried an aura of incompetence about him. He took down every detail of the episode, but did not seem to have any dramatic notions for the defense. ''We'll let the prosecution present the facts,'' he said.

''*Their* facts will wipe out Balook!'' Thor protested.

''That depends on interpretation,'' Twild said mildly.

''Interpretation!'' Thor shook his head unbelievingly. ''We can't interpret away that brat's death!''

Twild merely looked at him, unmoved.

Thor said no more. It was obvious that the miracle they had prayed for had not come to pass.

THOR WENT TO the stable to check on the *Baluchitheria.* As he entered, his tension and concern seemed to slide off. He felt at ease with the huge animals. It wasn't just Balook; Theria and Blooky accepted him too, and made no demands beyond what he freely gave. How much better this world of the ancient animals seemed than the complex, deadly world of the human species!

''I hope we can save you, Balook!'' he said.

He had arranged with Barb to have one of the two of them always with the animals, and the other watching the trial. That way they could be on top of both aspects of the situation. They had their radios, so they could keep in touch with each other, but it did mean that they were usually separated.

There were Project personnel here, by court injunction. Apparently the judge was afraid that an adult would find a way to spirit Balook away before the trial, in effect jumping bail. Of course that was nonsense; only Thor or Barb could make the animals travel. Therefore no one associated with the Project said a word; they remained clear, physically and legally, lest the local authorities catch on that the surest way to confine the animals would be to remove Thor and Barb. If the worst came—but they never discussed that.

All they really knew was that they were in the midst of love and death: the burgeoning love between the two of them, and the threatened death of the animal that had brought them together. It was a devastating combination, and trouble.

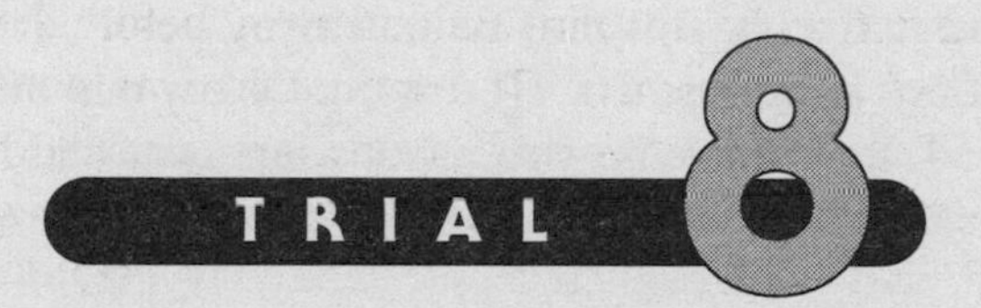

IT WAS AN old-fashioned jury trial. Most trials these days were handled by computer, dispensing with the complicated paraphernalia and rituals. The evidence was assembled and analyzed and the verdict presented in rapid order. The months-or years-long waits of the past were gone; the moment the cases were assembled, they were decided. But in special cases, the archaic system could be requested and invoked. This was as special as a case could get!

Barb sat in on the long, dull empaneling of the jurors, and radioed regular reports. Thor sat in the stable, watching the sightseers come and go. He had thought interest would slacken, but with the publicity of the trial it intensified. There were fewer children, more adults—and they came to stare at Balook. They seemed to be harder-eyed, less friendly. The death of the firecracker boy had transformed the atmosphere. Thor didn't like it at all.

"Twild is challenging every prospect," Barb said on the radio. "He asks them if they feel an animal who kills a man should be executed, and when they say yes, he dismisses them for cause. The judge doesn't like it, but can't stop it. But they're *all* saying yes!"

"They're against us," Thor said. "Now that the brat is dead, they think he was a poor innocent child, and Balook's a ravening monster. We can't get a fair trial here."

"That's what I think. The public is fickle; they saw Balook as a terrific curiosity at first, then they were mad at him, then when Mayor Caldwell set up the side-show they were positive, and now they've swung back the other way. I asked Twild why he doesn't petition for a change of venue, but he says that would not help, and not to worry."

"Sometimes I wonder which side he's on," Thor muttered.

"Twild is all we've got," Barb said dispiritedly. "I guess he knows what he's doing."

"He's nailing Balook's coffin!" Thor retorted.

She did not argue the case.

Later, the news got worse. "The judge has called a halt," Barb reported. "He says they've got to empanel a jury before he dies of old age, and that no more jurors can be disqualified for believing an animal that kills a man has to be killed."

"But that means a stacked jury!" Thor protested.

"Twild says he's made his point, and there are other ways to defend Balook."

"I hope so!" Thor said. "But is Twild looking for them?"

Again she did not answer.

Next day Thor took his turn in the courtroom. The jurors were there, and the prosecution presented its case. The lawyer for the State was a sharp young man with eloquent mannerisms, and seemed to know exactly what he was doing. Methodically he brought out witnesses to establish that Balook had run wild, had struck the boy, had stomped the car, had attacked the police floater and had fled the scenes of all these outrages.

"But I made him do it!" Thor protested to Twild. "I made him run, so he wouldn't smash any more cars, I made him attack the floater because it was shooting at us—"

"Were you in control when the boy was hit?" Twild asked him mildly.

"No, not then. He had been spooked by the firecracker and everything. But—"

"The prosecution's main case rests on that act. The rest is merely corroborative. All you could do would be to implicate yourself; you could not help the animal."

Thor shut up, chagrined. Twild was right; the boy was Balook's responsibility, and the rest was more or less irrelevant.

But there was no question about Balook's guilt in that one case. He *had* struck the boy, and that *had* been the cause of the boy's death. State experts were confirming that point now. Even Thor, if he should have to testify, would have to agree to that.

Yet Twild seemed unperturbed. What sort of defense did he have in mind—if any? Thor's stomach was beginning to hurt.

When the prosecutor finished presenting his case, it looked airtight. Balook had killed. The law was clear. Balook must die.

Desolate, Thor left the courtroom. The trial was not over, but it seemed that it might as well be.

NEXT DAY BARB took the courtroom again, while Thor perched on Balook, clinging like a lost soul to the huge neck. But it was the rhino's soul that was at stake. How lucky the animal was that he couldn't know the fate they were fashioning for him!

"Thor!" Barb said urgently on the radio. "Twild's putting on a good case. You should be here."

"How can I leave Balook? I may never have the chance to be with him again . . ."

"All right, I'll tell you. Twild's showing that it was an accident. Films prove Balook never even saw the boy. It's like a car hitting a pedestrian in the right of way. If the pedestrian was at fault—"

Hope flared. "Do you think it'll work?"

"Well, Twild is coming across with a lot more moxie than we expected. It seems pretty convincing. I think we underestimated him. Maybe that's the way he likes it."

But on cross-examination the prosecutor established that Balook did not have the right of way. He had stepped over the guide rope at the same time as he struck the boy; the guilty foot was across, the other forefoot caught behind the rope. The boy had been in the reserved channel, but had just gone out of it, and was just outside it when struck. Balook was technically at fault, not the boy.

"But the boy was dancing all around Balook's path!" Thor cried indignantly.

"Not at the moment he was struck," Barb said glumly. "The film shows he had just ducked under the rope. It's just chance, but that's the way it is."

So that defense had come to nothing. But Thor had to admit that it had been a good try. Had Twild carried it off, the charges against Balook would have had to be reduced. Maybe they *had* misjudged the man.

"I don't understand this," Barb said later. "Twild's putting in evidence a lot of data about the Project. How it was organized, how the rhino egg was modified, the number of failures. How the real rhinos were used to nurse—"

"I *know* all that!" Thor snapped. "What's the point?"

"That's what I'm *saying*!" Barb snapped back. "I don't see the point—but that's what he's doing."

"Well, I hope *he* knows what he's doing!"

"Ditto here."

In due course it became clear that Twild did know what he was doing. He made a strong case to show that the *Baluchitheria* were unique. There was no other grown male except Balook; no other female except Theria; no baby except Blooky. In all the world there were no others of this species, and had not been for millions of years. The diminished finances of the Project guaranteed that this would not be done again; the tide of experimentation had moved on.

Barb held the radio up so that it picked up the lawyer's words directly.

"Kill this animal," Twild said, his voice assuming

new authority, "and you are not punishing an individual entity, whatever his technical guilt may be." He made it sound as if the prosecution had made a lot of fuss about nothing. "You are eliminating a unique creature. One that can not be replaced. You are eradicating an entire species. You are committing genocide." The last word sounded unutterably foul.

"Genocide!" Thor echoed as he heard. "God, yes! There *is* no other Balook!"

It was a stroke of genius. There were laws against the taking of life unnecessarily, animal life included. There were stronger laws against taking the last life of a species. To kill a man was wrong; to kill *all* men was worse. To kill one *Baluchitherium* was permissible in certain circumstances; to kill the last *Baluchitherium* was not. The reason for the inability of the Project to create more members of this species might be as much political and economic as scientific; that did not matter. If Balook died, so would the species. No species could deliberately be rendered extinct. Not legally.

The perfect defense! Balook could have killed a hundred boys, yet be immune to execution. He was unique.

"Except for one thing," the prosecutor pointed out. Balook was not the only one of his kind. He was one of two males. The other was Blooky.

"But the species can't reproduce that way!" Thor objected. "Theria is Blooky's mother!"

He knew that Barb was shaking her head at the other radio. "Incest means nothing to animals—or man either, when it comes right down to it. They can reproduce—theoretically."

"But even if it were desirable to breed Blooky with

his mother when he grew up, she would by then be too old,'' Thor said.

''The court doesn't care about that,'' she returned darkly. ''There would be one male and one female left. Legally, Balook is expendable.''

Was Blooky's life to be the forfeit of Balook's? It seemed so, ironically.

Twild, seemingly undismayed, continued with another defense. He played up Balook's magnificence, his stature as an animal—and his limitations too. An animal could not comprehend murder; if he was dangerous, he should be restricted, not killed. A strong enough enclosure . . .

Thor thought about that. No ordinary enclosure could hold Balook when he really wanted to get out. They would have to build something like the Chinese Wall—and the Project no longer had the funds. Balook couldn't stand to be tethered; he would break any chain, or break his leg trying. Which meant they would have to hamstring him, so that he could never run again . . .

''No!'' Thor cried aloud. Balook would be better off dead!

To Barb he said: ''I'm going to have to talk with Twild. He doesn't understand Balook.''

''All right,'' she agreed dubiously.

Thor biked into town, using the machine he had rented for the duration. It was about as much as the Project could afford at the moment. It felt good to ride a bicycle again, and to share the paths with other bikers; it made him seem normal.

He reached town and quietly entered the courtroom.

Twild was showing slides of Balook, Theria and Blooky in various activities. They were magnificent animals, and Thor was sure the jury was being swayed. It would be easy to condemn a ravening monster, but hard to wipe out the magnificence of living *Baluchitherium.*

But before Thor had a chance to talk with Twild, a woman entered and approached Thor. She was middle-aged and undistinctive; he did not recall seeing her before, though it was possible she had been among the thousands of visitors to the stable.

"Mr. Nemmen," she whispered urgently. "You don't know me, but I went out to see your animals just now, and something's wrong. I think you'd better get out there, immediately."

"I just left them," Thor said, irritated. "They were all right. Balook remains weak, but is healing nicely."

"I mean the people," she said. "They're gathering a couple of kilometers away, carrying gasoline—I just happened to go by. When I saw that, I turned right about and drove here. Those beautiful animals—I'm afraid something's going to happen!"

"Gasoline!" Thor was shocked. He knew what gasoline was; it was an old-time fuel once used in motors. Now it had only specialized applications. It was highly flammable, and even explosive when ignited in confinement. If it were spread about the stable region and lit, there could be a terrible conflagration. "They're going to lynch Balook!"

"I don't know about that," the woman said. "But since that boy died, there's been strong feeling, and now that your lawyer's getting him off—"

"We can't be *sure*," Barb said. "It might be coincidence. Maybe an old-fashioned motor show—"

Thor doubted that. "Thanks for telling me!" he said to the woman. "I'll get right out there!"

"We aren't all chameleons in our feelings," she said. "I think the majority of us would be satisfied to see the rhinos exonerated, but there's a violent minority that knows no law."

He didn't even stop to see Twild. The woman was right: he had to check on it immediately. But Barb was right, too: he could not make any accusations until he was sure. If he cried "lynch" in court, and it was a false alarm—

He fairly sailed along the road, making the best time ever. He was lucky that there was little traffic, for he did not want others to note his mission. He reached the compound without event.

All was quiet. Only a few sightseers were there: a light day. The *Baluchitheria* were contentedly pulling down foliage in the pasture area. The trees of this region had been pretty much denuded below the nine meter level; soon the animals would have to be moved. No bad men were in evidence. Apparently it was a false alarm.

Still, he wanted to be sure. He poked around—and discovered a barricade blocking off incoming traffic. A sign said CLOSED FOR REPAIRS.

But the exhibition was not closed! The sign was a fake. It explained why there were so few visitors: as the earlier ones cleared out, they were not being replaced. But who had set it up?

He checked the area the woman had mentioned, hiding as well as he could in the brush. It was there: gasoline in assorted containers, as though many people had scrounged for it. There were hard-eyed men standing guard.

It added up. Get the sightseers out, then move in, dousing the stables with gasoline and setting them afire. Suddenly—no animals! And no proof, for the perpetrators would be gone as soon as the flames started.

But still he lacked proof. If he called the police, it could turn out that there really was an antique motor exhibit being set up nearby. He had to wait until the lynchers made their move.

At least he could prepare for it. If they were going to douse the stables with gasoline and burn them down, he could make sure the *Baluchitheria* could get out. No doubt the lynchers planned to make this seem like an accident; they would not shoot or do anything else to give themselves away. They would just sneak in, douse, light, and sneak out—while Balook burned. Then the outcome of the trial would be academic.

But they surely knew that the animals were always attended. Were they planning to burn Thor too? Somehow he didn't think so. It would not be because of squeamishness, for obviously these were completely unscrupulous characters. It was that a human death would bring a much more thorough investigation, and they couldn't risk that. No, they would probably try to lure him off on some spurious pretext.

How could he foil it? He had to remain with Balook, to guide him out, leading Theria and Blooky. If he tried to remain, they might shoot him with an anesthetic dart and bring him out unconscious anyway. In fact, they might do the same to the animals, to be sure they could not escape the fire by making desperate rushes. Mere darts could not put down Balook or Theria, but Blooky could succumb, and then the others might not leave. He had to play the seeming innocent—but then their plan would work!

First, he could notify Barb. Their radio was on a private channel, and coded, so the message was unlikely to be intercepted. "Barb, I think that woman's right. They're planning to lynch Balook!"

"I was afraid of that," she said grimly. "I'll call the authorities."

"But I don't have proof. We can't risk a false alarm. Not with the emotional climate here."

"We can't risk a lynching, either!" she retorted.

"Right. So I'll fasten my radio on Balook and leave it on. If you hear anything suspicious, you notify the authorities. Fast!"

"Why can't you just call me when anything starts?"

"I'm afraid it won't be obvious." Quickly he described what he had already observed. "So if anyone calls me away on some pretext—well, I've got to go along. I want to spring this trap now—or next time I may not have the chance."

"Why spring it at all? I think we're going to win this case! Twild is really bearing down now. If we can keep Balook safe—"

"That's it," he said. "*They* think Balook will get off in the trial, so they're going vigilante—just to make sure he dies. That's how mobs are. If they can't get their victim fairly, they'll get him unfairly. If one thing doesn't work, they'll try another. They're lawless zealots."

"I'd like to exterminate *them* instead of Balook!" she said darkly.

"Maybe we can do that! We've got a much better chance of stopping them if we spring their first trap, and foil it—and catch them in the act. *Then* they'll be exposed, and maybe confined, and Balook'll be safe."

"Sounds risky to me," Barb said. "Balook could get destroyed, if we don't stop them!"

"Don't I know it! But we've already seen that we can't just let justice take its course. We *won't* stop them unless we expose them. This is our best chance, because they don't know we know."

"Just the same, it's not worth Balook's life! I'm calling the police."

"No! That will scare off the lynchers and we won't catch them. Then they'll strike tomorrow or some other time, and the police won't believe us, and that'll be the end."

"I hope you're making sense to *you*, because you're not making much sense to *me*!"

"Just promise me you won't say a word—until we're *sure*."

She sighed. "All right, Thor. But I think it's a mistake."

"I'm fixing the radio now. I don't think anybody'll notice it here on Balook, and you'll be able to hear anything loud. If I have to, I'll just yell."

"Thor, be careful!" she said. "I don't like this at all. Balook's not the only one I care about, you know."

"I know. Theria and Blooky are at risk too. I hate it, but I've got to do it."

"Them too," she agreed.

"Right. Bye." He scrambled down Balook's back and let himself down by the tail.

Only when he hit the ground did the significance of her last comment register. She cared for Balook, Theria, Blooky—and whom? He felt a warm surge. To have his love for her returned—it was still so new that he tended to assume it wasn't so.

The stable doors could be barred from the outside, so as to contain the big animals. They were pretty solid; this was no longer the jury-rigged tent setup, but a prefabricated structure of surprising solidity. Balook might be able to crash out if he really tried, but Blooky certainly could not. Also, if the animals were dazed by anesthetic darts—there was pretty potent stuff available, he now remembered, so that even the largest animals were not entirely immune—they would not be able to make much of an effort.

He walked up to the doors and checked the barring mechanism. Could it be dismantled, so that the doors would not hold? Then the rhinos could get out quickly in an emergency.

Thor saw that there was no simple way to sabotage the bar; it had been designed to resist abuse. He would have to get a screwdriver and remove the big screws embedded in the door; then the framework would not hold.

He knew where the tools were: in a shed by the side of the stable. He headed for them.

A man was standing there. "Come with me, boy," the man said as Thor approached.

"Sorry, I'm busy," Thor said nervously.

"I insist." The man's hand shot out and grabbed Thor's upper arm.

Charged like a power cell, Thor exploded. He threw off the man's hand and punched him hard in the stomach. He was a good twenty kilograms lighter than the man, but he caught his opponent by surprise. Air whooshed out of the man's mouth and nose, and he bent forward. He had been struck—largely by accident—in the solar plexus, the central complex of nerves.

Fevered plans flitted through Thor's head as he saw the man stagger and struggle for breath. Knock him out, take his clothing, infiltrate the lynch network, subvert their plot . . . but he knew these were phantoms. The man's clothes wouldn't fit him, he couldn't knock the man out anyway unless he hit him on the head with a wrench, the lynchers would surely know each other by sight. Also, their plot was too direct to be subverted: dump gasoline on the stable, ignite it, scram.

So Thor did what came naturally. He grabbed his tools and sprinted back toward the stable. He'd have to break Balook out *now*!

The stable door was open. Had he left it ajar? He charged inside. "Barb! Barb!" he called loudly, so that the radio on Balook's neck would pick it up. "It's started! Call the police!"

Balook's head swung toward him. Then Thor saw the blood on the animal's neck. Just above that blood was a jagged mass of plastic and metal.

The radio had been smashed. Apparently someone had come in the door and fired a shot at the radio, and the impact had wounded Balook again.

But he had heard no shot, and Balook had not been spooked. How could that be?

A silencer! A device to make a gun relatively quiet, so as not to attract attention. Of course they would use something like that for this.

"Oh, Balook!" Thor cried. He jumped on the lowered head and scrambled up the neck.

The injury was minor; just a series of scratches and bruises and some lost hair. Nothing like the earlier wound, from which Balook was now almost wholly recovered. Best to let this one bleed, clot, and scab over; though the damaged area was several centimeters across, it was no more than a pinprick to Balook.

But the radio was a complete loss. He had no way to warn Barb. Whatever happened, he would have to fight it through on his own.

Thor sniffed, becoming aware of something. Balook sniffed too. "You can smell better than I can," Thor said. "What is that odor?" But of course the animal could not tell him.

The fumes became stronger. It was an odd, pungent smell, a little like new oil-base paint, but with less flavor. Thor was sure he had run across it before—but where, when?

He sniffed again, and again. Suddenly it came to him: an exhibit. And old-fashioned boat show, with sails and motorboats. The type of thing used before the modern electrics took over. Gasoline motors.

It was gasoline. He had known it was coming, but had seldom actually smelled it.

"We've got to *move*, Balook!" he cried, alarmed. "Go on out that door!"

But the door had swung closed. As Balook nudged against it, Thor realized the truth: they had been locked in. By the very bar he had sought to disable. While he had been checking the radio and Balook's wound, the trap had been closing. What an idiot he had been, to let it happen!

"Break it! Break it down, Balook!" Thor cried, urging the animal forward.

But Balook balked. It was not that he lacked the power; it was that he was normally a gentle animal, not given to destruction. They had encouraged that trait at the Project. In nature there could have been few if any predators on his kind; *Baluchitherium* was simply too big. It was easy for a big animal to be peaceful, if it had nothing to fear. Only for extremely pressing reason would Balook become violent. Therefore he could not understand Thor's urgings. Perhaps he assumed that Thor was directing him back, away from the door.

Then a new smell came: smoke. Someone had ignited the gasoline, and it was burning explosively, setting fire to the stable.

Balook could never have smelled such smoke before, but generations of rhinos had experienced prairie fires. The effect was electric: Balook snorted, and all his huge muscles tensed.

"Out! Out!" Thor cried. Now he was glad he was here with Balook, because at least he knew how to direct the rhino's great force.

This time Balook understood him perfectly. He ran at the barred door, put one massive front hoof forward, and struck it. This was the kind of motion Balook's kind must have used in the Miocene Epoch, to knock down small trees whose upper foliage remained too high to reach. Certainly it came naturally to the animal. The door burst apart, the bar fastenings snapping. What had there been to worry about! Thor, like the lynching party, had seriously underestimated the rhino's power. They were out.

Flames engulfed the stable. The gasoline must have been spread all around the outer walls. The smoke was awful: roiling black and red clouds of it rose into the sky.

"Theria! Blooky!" Thor screamed. "The other stables!"

Again, Balook understood, for this was natural to him. He charged the other stable, reared, and plunged both forefeet against the flaming wall. It was like a ten-ton battering ram, for most of Balook's weight was behind those hooves. The wall collapsed inward.

Thor choked on the awful smoke and buried his face against Balook's neck to shield himself from the heat. Balook had greater resistance, thanks to his insulative layer. The way had been cleared; now Theria and Blooky could get out.

But they didn't. "Move! Move!" Thor cried, and paused to cough. "The whole thing will collapse on us—"

But Balook merely stood, waiting for Theria—and Theria would not leave the burning building.

"For God's sake!" Thor cried. "What's the—"

Then he saw what was the matter. Blooky was tethered. He had been restrained while he wore the splint; the splint was now gone, and his broken leg healed—it had been a minimal break—but he was still restrained. He could not get away—and Theria would not leave without him.

Thor scrambled forward. "Down, Balook!" he yelled as he passed the animal's ear. Balook obligingly lowered his head, and Thor slid across the bent nose and dropped to the floor. He ran to Blooky and grabbed at the knots of the tether.

The job seemed interminable. Blooky wanted to get out; he was bucking about and bleating pitifully. That was what made it so hard. Thor didn't have a knife to cut the rope; he had to untie it. And he *couldn't*—not with this constant jerking.

Meanwhile, the heat was increasing, and both breathing and seeing were becoming harder.

"Balook!" Thor cried, and the animal came, trusting his friend to solve this riddle and get them out. "Take this rope in your teeth! Chew it, snap it!" He put the length up to Balook's fleshy lips.

But this was too complicated. Balook merely sniffed the rope inquiringly.

"Okay, then—your foot!" Thor cried. "Foot!"

Balook was familiar with this command, because of all the times he had had to lift his feet in turn for the farrier to trim the hooves. He lifted one forefoot, and Thor took advantage of a momentary slack in the rope to make a loop and pass it over the thick ankle. Then Blooky jerked away again, and the loop pulled tight. It

He thought the fire was chasing him

could not slip off, because of the enormous spread of Balook's hoof.

"Now break it!" Thor cried. "Kick, Balook, kick!"

Feeling the tether, Balook did just that. Balook had never been tethered; he tolerated no bindings. He backed off and yanked hard.

Blooky was hauled roughly across the floor. But the rope held. Instead, another section of the wall ripped loose. More fire flowed in.

But Blooky was now free of the wall—and tethered instead to Balook. "Run! Run!" Thor cried, unable to worry about the tether when the fire was closing in.

Blooky got up and ran. Theria followed. But that brought the loop tight about Balook's ankle again. As soon as he felt its restriction, he kicked again. Blooky was thrown to the floor a second time, his two hundred kilograms no match for Balook's power.

"God, he's going to be dragged to death!" Thor cried, horrified.

But this time the rope slackened as Blooky rolled over against his sire's foot. Thor leaped for it, enlarging the loop, letting it fall free. Blooky still was tied, but now the rope dragged loose.

Blooky got up and ran again, apparently unhurt. Balook followed. Theria followed Balook. And Thor was left behind.

He had no choice. He launched himself after Theria, grabbed her tail and hung on. Her moving hind legs battered him, but she hauled him out of the blazing building.

Now there was nothing to do but ride Theria. He hauled himself hand over hand up her tail. She could have dislodged him with a single kick, but was used to people climbing her tail. Barb looked like a softly feminine girl, which she was, but she had hefty muscles in her arms, as did Thor, because of this constant climbing exercise. Now he realized that the rope-climbing exercise he had done during his two year hiatus was because he wanted to return to his friend and climb his tail again. That much of his wish had come true.

He clutched the thick folds of Theria's skin over her hindquarters. This was an excellent way to get killed, mounting a moving rhino, but it was the only way. He scrambled to her back.

Theria did not like it. Now she realized that it was not her mistress on her back, and she was every bit as finicky as Balook about such details. But her concern for her calf distracted her, and she tolerated Thor with only minor twitchings of her skin.

Blooky, meanwhile, was desperately dragging the rope and one burning patch of wallboard. He was afraid to stop, though the weight might have been as much as a hundred kilograms, because he thought the fire was chasing him. Balook thought so too, and wanted to attack the fire—but every time he stomped it, the rope went taut and Blooky was jerked up short, cruelly. Theria hovered between the two, not knowing what to do.

Thor didn't know what to do either. The situation was uncomfortable, but at least they were moving away from the blazing buildings. He wanted to get far from the fire and the compound, because the assassins might be lurking with guns, ready to finish the job they had botched.

Whereupon he saw two men with guns. Balook charged them, and they scrambled to safety behind a tree without shooting.

Why *hadn't* they shot? Immediately, Thor thought of the answer: if they killed Balook here, they would have no way to move his twelve tons back into the stable, and their "accidental burning" would be discredited. A bullet was not a fire!

But he still had to do something, for soon the police, ignorant of the true nature of the fire, would be out after the *Baluchitheria.* How could Thor protect them, until he had a chance to explain? The average person was terrified by the sight of such huge animals on a seeming rampage.

It came to him in a marvelous flash: *he could take Balook to his own trial!* Surely the animal had the right to be represented in person!

The burning wall fragment sluffed off parts of itself, and the flame reached the rope. Suddenly the main mass was severed, and Blooky had only the length of tether to drag. One problem solved!

"Whoa, Balook!" Thor called, and Balook halted. Theria halted behind him, and Thor was ready to transfer. "Head down, Theria!" he called.

But he was not her mistress. She would not lower her head for him.

"Oh, good God!" he exclaimed. "Theria, you know me! All I want is to get off you and on Balook. Then everything'll be just fine. But you have to let me down."

That logic was too sophisticated for her. Obdurate, she stood.

"All right, I'll slide down your tail," Thor said, irritated. He moved back. But as he crossed her rump, still some four meters high, she gave a little stomp with one rear foot. Not a kick, just a minor gesture. He knew that gesture; he had seen it on occasion. It was her signal that she was losing her patience with indignities. Such as a stranger climbing down her tail.

Thor perched, exasperated. He could not ignore Theria's warning; she had a mind of her own, and about eight thousand kilograms to back it up. Beside Balook she looked relatively petite, but he could break his leg jumping down her side. She had to let him get down—and she refused.

But in due course, when she got sufficiently annoyed, she might simply throw him off. One irate sweep of her nose across her back would finish him. He could not afford to wait for that!

"Come on, brain—there must be *some* way!" he said, pulling at his hair as if to loosen the gray cells beneath.

Balook approached, sensing Thor's distress. He wondered why Thor was choosing to ride Theria instead of him. The big nose came to nudge Thor's shoulder. "Careful, Balook, you'll shove me off!"

Too late; Balook was used to nudging Thor when Thor was firmly planted on the ground, and a meter's worth of shove didn't matter. Here, it was disaster.

"Balook!" Thor cried as he lost his purchase. He flung out his arms to grab Balook's nose, his feet dangling helplessly between the two great animals.

Balook lowered his head slowly, as was customary when someone was riding it, and Thor's feet touched. But Thor did not let go. "I'm across!" he exclaimed, surprised. He scrambled on up the massive neck. Why hadn't he thought of it before?

"On, Balook!" he cried, rejuvenated. There was such a difference between mounts!

HE GUIDED BALOOK cross-country toward the town, until there was no alternative to the road. Then the parade pre-empted one lane of a car route. There was some commotion and staring, of course, but not nearly as much as the first time. Too many thousands of these people had seen the great rhinos; they were no longer such a novelty.

He located the court building and guided Balook up the broad pseudo-marble steps. Theria and Blooky followed dutifully.

Fortunately the court building was palatial: one of the town's few concessions to old-fashioned conspicuous grandeur. The main doors were ten meters tall, framed by gothic columns, and even the internal doors on the ground floor had clearances of seven meters. The court rooms had commensurate domed ceilings. It was as though it had been built with *Baluchitherium* in mind.

They tromped down the royal hall to the court room where the trial was being conducted. The door was closed, and Thor had no way to open it; he had to stay on Balook so as to guide him. "Push it open!" he cried, urging the rhino into it.

The door did not open. Instead it tore off its hinges and slammed down to the floor beyond. There was a collective gasp from the audience inside as Balook burst into the chamber.

The judge and jury turned amazed faces toward the animals. As Balook strode into the center of the chamber, judge, jury, bailiffs and lawyers scrambled unceremoniously for the far side. This was just as well, because by the time Thor managed to bring Balook to a halt the judge's bench had been overturned. The rhino was not used to precise maneuvering within a building.

"We've only come to attend our own trial!" Thor called. "They tried to lynch Balook . . ."

He thought it was a moment of triumph, but suddenly he realized that he had made a ghastly mistake. The lawyer for the defense, Twild, looked horrified. Twild might have been well on the way to winning the case, but that was over now. Both judge and jury were staring at the monstrous animals with shock, fear and revulsion. Nothing, now, would convince them that Balook was just a harmless, misunderstood animal.

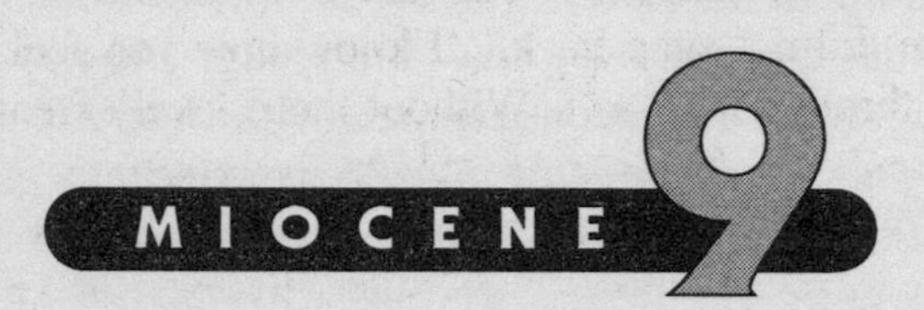

THE JURY WAS out, the rhinos were in new temporary stables, and Thor was under virtual house arrest. Because there really *had* been a fire, and Thor had no apparent motive to have started it, he had not been formally charged with breach of the peace. But while the arson investigation was going on, he was restricted.

The worst of it was, he was separated from Balook. The judge had noted that all of the trouble Balook had gotten into in this region had been while Thor was with him. Again, there was no formal charge, but Thor was forbidden to join Balook until the facts had been ascertained to the judge's satisfaction. The judge, it seemed, was not an easy man to satisfy.

Barb tried to cheer him, but there was little anyone could do to alleviate his gloom. He had been apart from Balook for so long, and then so actively rejoined, and now to be apart in the hour of crisis—the distress drove him relentlessly. He lost his appetite, he had trouble sleeping, and his entire existence seemed bleak and meaningless.

"Is there anything I can do?" Barb asked worriedly.

"No!" he snapped. "Just leave me alone!"

She did not snap back. "I know how you feel. I've been through it myself. Without thosc lovely creatures, we aren't anything." She moved to the door.

Thor looked up. "You *do* understand," he said. "Balook means more to me than anything. More than you. I guess you could hate me for that—"

"Or love you," she said. "If you aren't true to your first loyalty, what else is worth anything? If you didn't love Balook, and I didn't love Theria—"

"There wouldn't be anything between the two of us," he finished. "I guess most people would forget about the animals—"

"Don't ever do that!" she exclaimed. "*Then* I'd hate you!"

"I'm sorry I snapped at you," he said. "There *is* something you can do for me. Two things."

"I know them both," she said. "First—" She pulled his head down and kissed him.

"That was one," he agreed.

"Second, I'll go talk to Balook for you."

He nodded. "Tell him I miss him."

"I will. Third—"

"Third? You're not going to try to break me out of here!"

"A gift for you. I thought it might help."

"A gift?" He took the small package she presented.

"A statue of Balook—maybe."

"Maybe?"

"That's right. Bye." She departed.

He opened the package. It was a block of brown tallow.

Thor shook his head. "A statue of Balook?" he asked the air, baffled.

The box said SCULPTOR'S WAX.

Then Thor smiled. A statue—if he could make it! What better way to spend his lonely hours, than to fashion a replica of his best friend, Balook. It would certainly give him something to do—something that was both a challenge, for he had never tried sculpting before, and a blessing, for the effort would surely occupy him for many hours.

There was an instruction leaflet in the box. It told how this hard wax would soften when warmed by human hands, so that it could be worked. It could also be carved by a knife. But its main property was its ability to melt away cleanly when subjected to appropriate heat, leaving no residue. Thus it could be used as the base for the "lost wax" process of metal sculpture. This was a method by which the wax carving was enclosed in a kind of cast, and the cast was heated, and the wax melted and flowed out a hole, leaving only its shape inside the cast. Then the hot metal was poured in, and cooled and solidified, and the cast was broken open. Result: a metal sculpture just like the original wax one. Few sculptors actually carved metal these days; wax was easier, and of course this process made it possible to make many replicas.

Thor was abruptly fascinated. A metal statue of Balook! Why not? He could have it with him forever, even if—

He stifled that thought. Balook had to live, somehow!

He took out the block of wax and ran his hands over it. The surface did soften, but not much. This was not clay, that could be scooped and kneaded readily!

He took the knife that came with the set and carved a shaving from a corner. It was not wood, either, or soap. It had its own texture, distinct from anything else. It was intriguing, but took time to adjust to.

Well, he would just have to plan his statue carefully, so as not to have to make any change in the main mass of wax. Part carving, part molding—it could be done, with patience. The great mass of the torso here, and the head here, and the legs—no, he'd better do them separately, and attach them after the rest was done, so that they would not break. And the head—attach that too. Otherwise there would be too much wax wasted, and the figure would be smaller than it had to be.

Thor contemplated the wax for some time, judging how to use it economically, figuring out ratios. He tried to visualize the form within it: a rhino waiting to be expressed. Balook, in miniature, as if seen through a window. At last he decided he could make a statue six inches tall at the shoulder—inches, not centimeters—for a ratio of one inch to three feet. Skip would love such a ratio, for he used the archaic measures. Thor did not, but it just didn't work out so neatly in the metric system. He needed something simple, so that he could match it up readily by eye, and not have to bother with fractions. An inch a yard was simple. Call it an inch a meter, a compromise between systems. Just as Balook himself was a compromise between epochs.

First he had to carve out the main torso, headless and legless. But he had to do it in such a way that the head could be conveniently formed from the largest cut-out chunk of wax.

He assessed the situation, reconsidered, judged, and decided that his assessment was good. He proceeded to the carving, using first the knife for the broad outlines, then a dental pick Barb brought him for the finer work. The hours passed like phantoms.

The body took shape, seeming almost to form itself from the wax. The separate head assumed character, guided by the same imperative. The legs began as crude sticks of wax, but became four stout, sculptured columns; he carved each to its proper proportions before attaching any. He made the tail similarly, and set it similarly aside.

Now he focused on the detail of the head, making the ears perk up, the nostrils flare, the lips part. He drew down the folds of skin at the neck, and made the lines around the eyes. The character of Balook emerged from the wax, as if Thor were merely cleaning away a covering on the figure that had been present all the time.

When all seemed right, he commenced the job of assembly. The head and neck attached to the body, and the line of their joining disappeared. The legs and tail attached to their respective moorings while the statuette lay on its side; the wax was stiff enough to maintain them this way without bending. He secured them as well as he could; it would not do to have Balook weak on his feet!

At last he stood the assembled statue on its legs.

But of course the rhino could not talk

They were uneven; he had to make adjustments. He made them, getting the footing firm. He removed his hands, and the statue stood alone for the first time.

The figure of Balook seemed to waver. Thor shook his head violently. He couldn't fall asleep now; it was almost finished!

But soon it wavered again. ''Balook, stand still!'' Thor exclaimed. ''How do you expect me to fix your foot when you keep moving about?''

Balook twitched his skin indifferently.

"I wish you could talk," Thor said. "We'd have such a conversation!"

But of course the rhino could not talk. Instead he reached up for a branch and tore it down with one good wrench of his neck. There was a small scar on that neck, where the smashed radio had been, and another on the belly.

"Balook, we've got to go away. Far away. Where they can never catch us."

The animal merely browsed.

"Come *on*." Thor walked beside him, tugging urgently at a fold of skin on the leg. "We don't have much time."

Now Balook paid attention. Thor guided the huge hornless rhino through the big trees. Slowly the nature of the vegetation changed, and Thor headed directly into that change, still on foot, still leading Balook.

The terrain became marshy, with many water plants. Balook didn't like it; his huge bulk needed solid footing. "Right; we'll turn back," Thor said. "Look for a way around this bog."

Abruptly he stopped. Before them, rooting in the soil, was the strangest elephant Thor had ever seen. It had a normal proboscidean or elephantine body and head—but its trunk was so broad and flat it was as though the creature had been squashed by some horrendous accident. Its lower jaw was almost as long as the trunk. The two tusks, though about half a meter long, were dwarfed. Two tremendous shovel-like teeth projected from the tip of that jaw.

Thor was back, away, and up on Balook's back before the first shock faded. Then he suffered a second shock, less horrendous, more profound. The shock of recognition.

This was no elephant, but a weird extinct offshoot he had seen illustrated in paleontology texts. *Platybelodon*—a swamp-rooting relative.

A contemporary of *Baluchitherium*, in the Miocene Epoch.

He remembered Barb's reference to her dreams about Theria. About going back to the Miocene Epoch, meeting *Baluchitherium*'s contemporaries. That was what he was doing now—with a vengeance!

Did Balook see the same thing?

From up on Balook's shoulder, Thor did not find the *Platybelodon* as imposing. It stood perhaps three and a half meters tall at the shoulder. He seemed to remember that they got larger later in the epoch. Anyway, they weren't aggressive. After looking briefly at Thor and Balook, the creature went back to its foraging. It used the two great front teeth to slice through water, vegetation and turf with singular dispatch, scraping up huge mixed mouthfuls that it then strained and sorted in its mouth. Its tongue, tusks and long lips separated solid from liquid, and organic from inorganic with marvelous facility. Watching it operate, Thor almost felt his own mouth watering for a taste of rich swamp muck.

Actually, it was not so strange to see this elephantine cousin foraging in the swamp. The elephants had been swamp-dwellers first, and had gradually moved to drier pastures as the climate changed and the swamp dried out. Some of them had even become mountain dwellers, in America; those had survived almost until the coming of the white man. Their extinction was theoretically a mystery; actually man was responsible, as with so many other innocent species. Man was the worst scourge to come upon the animal kingdom since the devastation of the dinosaurs. It was a mistake to assume that the present distribution and habitat of any species represented its paleontological evolution. There had once been woolly mastodons and woolly rhinos, as well as the tropical species.

Just as there had once been very large hornless rhinos like Balook. Could man also have—?

No, that was before man's time. That was one crime Thor's species could not be charged with. That was a relief!

They moved on, skirting the swamp. Thor swatted a mosquito; the insects did not seem to have changed much! He saw birds flitting through the foliage. He was no ornithologist, but they seemed familiar too, at least in general type. So did the trees and plants. All of which fitted together: the insects had evolved with the flowers, and the birds that preyed on insects followed right along.

Now the forest thinned. Piglike animals trotted out of Balook's way, unhurriedly. There was a snarl, and Thor saw a cat with tusks: a sabertooth. It had been ready to pounce on a porcine straggler, being hidden downwind, until Balook had disturbed the herd. No wonder the big feline was angry!

Farther along there was a huge dog, stout and muscular. In fact it was a bear-dog, for the bears had not quite separated from the canines in the early Miocene, and the raccoons had only just branched off. Thus these doglike carnivores were a very broad and important group.

Thor felt nostalgia for this world that had existed twenty million years before he was born, and faded ten million years ago. Balook's world . . .

"Let me down," Thor said. "I want to touch this realm, to experience it directly."

Balook obligingly lowered his head, and Thor climbed down. He walked among the trees, just looking and breathing. Behind him, Balook reached up to crop a high branch.

There was a surly grunt. Thor stopped. Before him a pig stood at bay—but what a pig! It was about one and two thirds meters tall at the shoulder, and three long. Thor placed it: *Entelodon*, another Old World Oligocene specimen. Part of Balook's world, of course. The trouble was, the monstrous swine was making ready to charge!

The pig advanced. Thor retreated. Those tusks were not large, in proportion, but the animal itself was so big that Thor wanted no part of it. He scooted back to where Balook stood.

But Balook was gone. He had wandered away, browsing. It had not occurred to him that there could be any threat to his small friend; after all, there was none to Balook.

Now this Oligocene-Miocene world seemed less delightful, more menacing. The huge pig had given up the chase, satisfied to have driven the intruder away from its territory. But what other animals were roaming nearby?

Thor hurried nervously along the trail of broken

branches and hoofprints Balook had left. He had to catch up! With Balook he would be safe, for the rhino had no natural enemies here. Alone, Thor was in trouble, for there were many pigs and saber-toothed cats and bear-dogs ready to do him in.

How could Balook have gone so far? It had been only a few minutes!

A few minutes! Thor remembered the chase he had made on the bicycle, when Balook had winded Theria and traveled across the countryside to join her. Balook could *move*, when he chose!

He burst into a glade, and almost under the tusks of something huge. Another elephant, or *Platybelodon*—no, it was yet another variation. These tusks pointed downwards and back, as though the creature's jaw had been turned upside down. This was *Dinotherium.* He remembered that these creatures had achieved enormous size—over four meters tall at the shoulders—second only to *Baluchitherium.* But that was later, in the Pliocene Epoch; this one was only three meters. Still too big for comfort!

Thor retreated, and the elephantoid did not pursue. These herbivorous animals who had never known man were basically peaceful; they only *looked* horrendous! Still, he would not want to cross one during mating season, or debate territory with it. Thor was struck by the complete similarity of the bodies of these creatures, with only their jaws and tusks differing; it was as if an elephant had interchangeable heads. Yet it was much the same for man; the basic human body had been perfected before the head, so that *Australopithecus*, Neanderthal, Cro-Magnon and modern man could be

He walked among the trees, just looking
and breathing

distinguished only by their heads. And not always then!

On he went, past numerous deerlike animals: "even-toed" ungulates, ancestors to the cattle, sheep, goats and modern deer. Still he did not find Balook. Belatedly he realized why: he had been following the trail of broken branches, but in this framework many large animals fed on the trees. Any of the elephant types could have done the damage. Balook might be far away, his trail having diverged long ago.

Now Thor really was lost.

He forced himself to stop running. He reminded himself that he was not really threatened here. There was hardly anywhere in the world, in all its history, where a man could not have walked with fair security. Few animals attacked man, and fewer could overcome him.

He peered through the forest, and saw a line, strung up high. He went to it.

Sure enough: it was the power line. The same one he had stayed under when they had fled the city. Oasis of peace!

No wonder he was breathless. He had come all the way out here on foot. But his running could not avert Balook's fate. If only there really were a hiding place, here in the thousand kilometer narrow oasis of vegetation!

Then he saw it. Not only the power line, but the thing it stood for. More than high voltage electric current, more than an advanced technology world.

He saw Balook's salvation.

If only he could make the authorities understand in time . . .

But at the moment he had a more immediate problem. He had evidently dozed off, or gone into some kind of trance, and wandered in a realm of his own making, of fantasy. A realm where Balook was safe! In the process he had not only deluded himself, he had violated his restriction, and would be in trouble with the court.

How had he done it? Surely there were guards or something in the building who should have challenged him! And the city—was it possible for him to have sleepwalked through that unobserved? And the time—he could not have come this far in the few minutes he had been afoot!

Ah, but he had been riding Balook! The rhino could have traveled that distance; after all, he had done it before.

Except that Balook was confined to the compound. It had been the scale model statue of Balook Thor had mounted. That of course was even less likely.

There was only one answer: he had fallen asleep, and was still dreaming. That dream had brought him to the answer that must have been lurking beneath his consciousness.

All he had to do was wake up.

With that realization, he relaxed—and fell into a deeper sleep.

HE WOKE AT the sound of the door. He was lying on his bunk beside the statue. Blearily he looked up. Barb was there, her face tragic.

That could mean only one thing. "They found Balook guilty?" he asked.

"Of manslaughter," she agreed. "They have sentenced him to—"

"To death," he said. That was the penalty for an animal who killed a man, whatever the circumstances.

Suddenly his revelation of the night seemed inadequate. He had been looking for a way to convince the jury and the public that there was a place for Balook in the contemporary world. Perhaps there was—but the decision had come too soon. Now it was too late to present his idea, too late to make the jury understand.

While Thor had slept, Balook had lost.

Now Barb saw the completed statue in wax, standing there so proudly. "It's beautiful!" she breathed—then sank down, sobbing.

Thor got up and put his arms around her, trying to comfort her. But it was a hollow effort. They both knew that Balook was done for.

Then Thor's eye fell again on the statue of Balook. It seemed to waver. Was he going back into his dream?

No, it was just a reminder of the revelation he had suffered during that vision. Maybe there was still a chance!

"Barb," he said into her fluffy hair.

She lifted her tear-wet face. "I'm sorry; I shouldn't have—"

"I have a crazy notion."

She paused, considering. "Not here. Not now."

That made *him* pause. What was she thinking of? "A way to save Balook."

"How I wish!" she said fervently. "But I just don't see how."

"Balook showed me, in a dream. Only they decided

against him too fast. But maybe it will work anyway. Can you get Twild to get a stay of execution?''

"I can try. But what—''

"I'd better not tell you. I don't want you to get in trouble if it doesn't work. But you can help. I'm locked up here, but you aren't.''

"Do you really have a way?'' she asked, daring to hope.

"I think so. It's wild and bold, but it might work. First I'll need a map—''

"A map of what?''

Thor did some fast thinking, his options expanding. "Maps of everything! An atlas!''

"An atlas! What does that have to do with saving Balook?''

"Everything, maybe! And a telephone.''

"They'll monitor any calls you make, and intercept anything long distance,'' she warned.

"Local is fine. And some research. Or a book on electro-magnetic waves.''

"Are you teasing me?'' she demanded.

"No, honest! It all connects. But we've got to act immediately.''

"I'll do what I can,'' she said, looking doubtful.

In a few minutes she fetched him a telephone and the first map she could find: one of the local county, including an expanded street directory of Eagle Stream. It was useless for his purpose, but he thanked her anyway. "But if you can find an atlas too—and the information on—''

"I'll try, Thor,'' she said, perplexed. She departed again.

Thor checked his watch. It was noon; he had slept the night, and had not yet eaten, but wasn't hungry. If this only worked!

He turned on the phone. "The power company," he said.

The screen flickered. Then a plush front office showed. "May I help you?" the decorative secretary inquired dulcetly.

"I'd like to talk to the president of the company, please," Thor said.

She did not crack a smile. "Do you have an appointment?"

"No, I'm just calling in."

"I am sorry, but Mr. Turrell requires an appointment. I can make one for you—" she checked her listings "—next Thursday at eleven fifteen. Will that be suitable? If you will give me your name and the nature of your business—"

"That's too late!" Thor protested. "I need to talk to him now!"

She frowned. "Is it an emergency?"

"Yes! It's a matter of life and death!"

"In that case perhaps an exception can be made. Now your name is—"

"Thor Nemmen. It's about Balook. The *Baluchitherium* who's on trial."

"Yes, I have seen that on the news," she agreed. "But surely you realize that Mr. Turrell has no business with—"

"Please, just let me talk to him. He can save Balook's life!"

Her mouth tightened, but her voice remained calm.

"I shall query his office." There was a brief pause; then she said: "Mr. Nemmen wishes to speak with you now, Mr. Turrell. He has no appointment. It's about the big animal that's been in the news; he says you can save its life."

The response was so vehement that even Thor could hear it, though it was not on his line. "That animal tore up our corridor! Thousand dollars' worth of damage! Deserves to be put away! Don't bother me again with such nonsense!"

The woman glanced up at Thor. "I am sorry; Mr. Turrell declines to speak with you. Have a nice day." She faded from the screen.

Stunned, Thor turned off the phone. He had put all his hopes on this contact, and it had soured before it started. What was he to do now?

He gazed at his statue of Balook. Again it wavered, as if trying to come to life. It would not let him give up.

He knew, intellectually, that he had worked so long without sleep that he remained behind, even after the night. His fatigue was making his vision blur, and probably distorting his judgment too. Even so, that statue compelled him. He had to act!

So the president of the power company wouldn't talk to him. What he needed to do was go there in person and barge into the man's office and make him listen! But it was folly to think he could do that; he couldn't even get out of this room without being challenged; the judge was keeping him confined until the business was done, and the business was the destruction of Balook.

Of the tiny Miocene Epoch enclave in the contemporary world.

He looked at the only other thing he had. The map of the county. It, too, wavered. Then he saw how he could use it.

He spread it out and pored over it, tracing the route of the power line corridor. Yes—there was where Balook had foraged, before the pursuit caught up. And there was the power company, well out of town but within the county boundaries. The line passed through it, skirted the town, and went on to the next county. It was part of a grid that covered the continent. Each local company produced its own electricity, but all were linked, so that if one or several failed, the power came across from the others. Thus the local company could drop offline, and the power was never interrupted. In that sense, the connecting lines were more important than the company. That was what he counted on.

He focused on the town. Here was the court building, and here was the building in which he himself was being held prisoner. They didn't call it that, of course; he wasn't under arrest, just in protective custody. But they would not let him out until too late.

He checked another region. Here was the compound where Balook and Theria and Blooky were being held. It was a thickly wooded region outside of town, which was just as well, because they had to let the rhinos feed, and they could destroy trees in short order if there were not enough of them available. That was part of what the townsmen had against Balook: the damage to local trees. Thor couldn't really blame them for that. But if that fool capering brat had not started it all, the rhinos would have been through the town and gone without significant damage to the local foliage.

He continued to pore over the map, virtually memorizing the key aspects of it. Instead of being useless, this was now exactly what he needed!

Barb returned. "I couldn't get a book on electromagnetism, but here's an atlas," she said. "Now will you tell me exactly what you are going to do with it?"

"No. It's not safe for you to know. But you can go to the library and look up the information there. Did you get the stay of execution?"

"Twild says he's appealing the decision, because the jury was biased. Remember, the judge overruled him on the matter of killing animals. That's why he didn't take it hard at the time; he knew he could use it to challenge the legitimacy of the trial if he lost. He's a lot sharper than we thought. So the execution's on hold until there's a decision on the appeal; if they turn it down, then Balook's done for, but Twild says it should keep things in stasis for several days. Is that enough?"

"Should be, if my notion works. If it doesn't, then no time's enough. How fast can you get the electromagnetic information? I don't need everything, just the health hazards of the waves."

"Thor, if you'd only tell me why—"

"I don't dare, Barb. I want to keep you innocent, so you can honestly tell them you had no idea what I had in mind. That should keep you out of jail."

"Thor Nemmen!" she exclaimed indignantly. "If you're going to do something that gets you in jail, I want to be with you!"

"That would be fun, but I don't think they'd allow

it. Anyway, you need to be with Theria and Blooky, if—"

The reminder struck her visibly. She looked as if she were about to cry, but she headed it off by grabbing his head and kissing him savagely instead. Then she hurried out.

Thor thought to use the phone to order himself a lunch. His appetite was returning. If he was as busy as he thought he might be, he wanted to be well fortified.

While waiting for it to arrive, he sauntered to the window and looked out. He made it seem casual, because it occurred to him that he might be under observation.

The window was fastened by a simple clasp. He opened it, and the breeze wafted in. He glanced down.

He felt dizzy. He was on the fourth storey, and the face of the building was completely blank except for the other windows—and all of them were closed, and set flush with the wall. There was no way for him to climb down, or even to scramble to another window. If he tried, he would fall to the concrete below, which was a good ten meters. So much for his notion of escape by that route!

But he knew he would not be able to do it by the door either. There would be laser guards set across it, or across the hall outside, invisible but certain to trigger the alarm.

Well, as long as the stay remained on Balook's execution, he could afford to bide his time. Maybe he would find some other way to escape.

He closed the window and returned to the map and statue. Then his meal arrived. He and the statue studied the map again while he ate. Then he got into the atlas, tracing the routes of the power lines that crisscrossed the continent. They were everywhere; there must be hundreds of thousands of kilometers of lines. That was excellent for his purpose.

Late in the day Barb returned. "I got some information on the electromagnetism," she said. "But Twild says the appeal may be decided much faster than usual, because of the notoriety of this case. It could be denied tomorrow."

"They're so eager to kill an innocent animal!" Thor said.

"Your crazy notion," she said urgently. "How can I help?"

Thor realized that he would have to tell her, at least partially. "I didn't want to involve you. I—I have to get to talk to the president of the power company. He can save Balook, if he wants to, and I think he'll want to, if I can only get him to listen. But he won't talk to me by phone. So I have to get there, brace him personally so he can't hang up. That means I've got to make a jailbreak. If you can find a way to turn off the laser alarms tonight—"

"I don't think I can, Thor. I don't know anything about electronics, except what I learned in the library today. There *is* a health hazard, but the power companies cover it up—"

"That's what I thought. That's what I'm counting on."

"Counting on!" she exclaimed indignantly. "What on earth are you talking about?"

"It won't count for anything if I can't get out of here! Isn't there some way?"

She became thoughtful. She walked to the window and looked out. "Maybe there is."

"I can't climb down from the window," he said. "Even if I hung a sheet out and climbed down it, I'd still be way too high for a safe fall. But if you could get me a long, strong rope—"

"I'll see," she said. "Keep alert after dark."

"What do you—?"

"I'd rather keep you innocent, so you can say you didn't know about it," she said, smiling wickedly.

"But I've got to know, so—"

She cut him off with a kiss. Then she left.

Thor stifled his mixed emotions. After all, she was only doing back to him what he was doing to her. Tit for tat.

He could not settle down to rest, so he made the assumption that he would get out, and rehearsed his actions and speech once he got to the power company. He would probably have to go there on foot, as there might be an alert out for his borrowed bike. That way he could hide better. Then, in the morning, he could sneak into the president's office and catch him there. The man would not be eager to listen, so Thor's case had to be good. It *was* good, but his presentation had to bring out its potential. He would have to capture Mr. Turrell's attention at the outset, and hold it until the logic registered. Until the man saw how the Miocene related to modern times. Balook's life depended on it.

AN HOUR AFTER dark, he heard a commotion outside. There was distant shouting, and the sound of vehicles accelerating, and a kind of crashing. What was going on?

A distraction, he realized. Barb must have arranged something, so that no one would notice when he went out the door, triggering the alarms!

He hurried to the door—and found it locked. They were taking no chances with him! How could he open it before the distraction faded? He had no tools, and the door was too solid for him to break down barehanded. Desperately he cast about; his gaze passed the window—

And saw a familiar shape in the mixed night lights of the town. Balook!

He dashed to the window and opened it. Balook was coming down the street, looming high in silhouette against the lighted windows of other buildings. What a sight that was—like a nightmare, only the monster of the night was his friend, and he was the monster's friend. Barb had broken him out, and now Balook was coming to break Thor out; *that* was her secret strategy!

But he couldn't get through that door! Was it all to be wasted? And what would happen when the townsmen rallied from their surprise and organized an effective pursuit? There was no way they could escape cleanly and be free.

He stared out the window, his emotions warring with each other. Part of him wished that this total foolishness could somehow work, and save them all. The rest knew it was disaster that could put all of them in deeper trouble than before. How could Barb have acted so rashly? She really wasn't the type!

No, obviously she *was* the type, for here was Balook. She was a lot like Thor himself, temperamental, yielding to the passion of the moment, willing to undertake desperate measures when the life of one she loved was threatened. She was the only other living person who cared about the *Baluchitheria* the way Thor did. He understood that aspect of her perfectly. But that meant that she could get into just as much trouble as he. They really *could* both wind up in prison—but probably not in the same cell.

Balook was charging on during Thor's amazed ponderings; the great rhino was at home in the darkness. He came up to the building, his head reaching up almost to Thor's level. "Balook!" Thor cried, heedless of all else in his joy at this momentary reunion with his friend.

There was noise behind him. Someone was at the door, still locked. Friend or foe?

Now a second rhino came up. Theria—with Barb aboard. "Thor!" she cried. "Mount! Mount!"

"But—" he protested, appalled. How could he—?

The door opened. Men jammed into the room.

"Here!" Thor called to Balook. "Reach here!"

Balook's head came up, seeking the familiar voice. Now it was only a meter below the level of Thor's floor. Thor scrambled out the window, hung on, let his feet dangle, then dropped.

He landed on Balook's massive head. The head lowered with the added weight, but was in no trouble. Thor scrambled to catch hold of folds of skin, and then backed down the neck to the solid shoulder. Now he was ready to ride!

"Lead the way!" Barb called. Her hair was flaring wildly as she rode Theria; she looked primitive and lovely.

Thor kicked Balook, directing him down the appropriate street. The map was clear in his head; he could take them right to the power station. It had to be fast, before the townsmen rallied. Balook was fresh, having recovered during the trial, and ready to run.

They charged through the town, avoiding those few cars and bicycles that were abroad. Soon they were in the country, the wind gusting past. There seemed to be no organized pursuit, only the lights of a few cars that remained a discreet distance behind. Perhaps they were only tracking the rhinos, so that a party could close in on them by day.

Well, he could take care of that. Once they got clear of the suburb, they could leave the road and cut through a forested region. The cars would have trouble following there.

They coursed on through the diminishing settlement.

Trees became more common. Balook seemed to understand that his life was at stake; he did not pause to snatch foliage, and maintained a swift pace, his feet handling the darkness well. Theria followed, with Blooky scrambling to keep up. It was like old times, except that times never had been like this, charging through the night as a family.

How had Barb broken them out? She must have opened the gates, then led the way with Theria, and by the time the authorities caught on, it was too late. Who would have suspected Barb of such a thing? Thor felt a warm surge of feeling; she was certainly the girl for him!

But first he had to do his part, and that was no easy thing. His strategy was a desperation ploy, and not just because of this second breakout of the rhinos.

Balook's ears perked. There was something ahead. Had the police set up a roadblock?

Then Thor saw it: a tiny figure standing in the road. A child! That was all they needed: another mischievous brat, like the one that had started all this. "Get out of the way!" Thor yelled.

But the child remained unmoving, even as Balook approached and came to a halt, looming tremendously over. It was a boy of about five years, in pajamas, standing with his arms outspread and his eyes screwed tightly shut. He looked terrified.

Theria drew up beside Balook. "What's a child doing out here alone at night?" Barb called.

"He must be lost," Thor called back.

"We can't just leave him here!"

"We can't just pick him up and take him along, either!"

Then Blooky, curious, moved forward. He had been petted by many children recently, and had lost his shyness with them. He sniffed the boy, then nuzzled him, hoping for a biscuit.

The boy jumped and opened his eyes. He stared at Blooky. Then, hesitantly, he reached out to pet the baby rhino on the nose.

Meanwhile, Thor was dismounting. Balook lowered his head, and Thor slid down his neck in the fashion of a banister, and finally across his broad nose and to the ground. "Who are you?" he demanded of the boy. "What are you doing here?"

The boy's mouth worked. "F-Fudgie," he said after a moment.

"That's your name?"

Gravely, the child nodded.

"Where's your home?"

The boy turned and pointed. There was a small side road that intersected at this point; Thor had not noticed it before, in the darkness.

"Your house is down that road?"

Fudgie nodded again. He was shivering.

"You had better go back home," Thor said. "It's cold and dangerous out here at night."

The boy nodded affirmatively, but made no motion toward his home.

Barb joined them. She knelt and put her arms around the child. "You're freezing!" she exclaimed.

"We can't stay here," Thor said urgently. "They'll have cars surrounding us!"

"Why are you here?" Barb asked the boy.

This time he answered intelligibly. "To meet the monster."

"The monster rhino?"

He nodded yes.

"Well, these are the rhinos, all right," she agreed. "But now you must go home before your folks miss you."

"Can't."

Thor saw a set of headlights approaching slowly from ahead. "They're coming! We've got to get off the road!"

"But the child!" she protested, for the boy was now clinging to her. "He could get run over in the dark!"

"Then bring him along!" Thor snapped.

She pondered only an instant. "Yes, we'd better. For one thing, it's warm on the rhinos. But I can't lift him up alone. We'll have to go on Balook. You take one hand; I'll take the other."

"But—" Thor started.

"Hurry!"

Bemused, Thor took one of the boy's arms. "Ready, Balook!" he called.

Balook brought his head low. Thor climbed on the nose, bracing himself by an ear. Barb followed, anchoring on the other ear. The rhino's ears were relatively tiny, but tough; they made excellent footholds and handholds. Between them they hauled up the boy, who straddled Balook's forehead.

"Up, Balook!" Thor said.

The head lifted. The boy whined with fright and screwed his eyes closed again.

When they were up, Thor left the boy in Barb's grasp and slid to Balook's shoulder. Then he hung on with one hand, reached forward with the other, and got hold of the boy's free arm. Barb let go, and Thor hauled the boy in to him. Then Barb slid down.

Now they were all at the broad shoulder. Thor was behind, Barb ahead, and the boy securely between them.

"Hang on," Thor said. "We're taking evasive action!" He kicked Balook, directing him nonverbally.

Balook turned and plunged into the forest at the side. Theria immediately followed, and of course Blooky followed her. In a moment they were out of sight of the road, and the vehicles were unable to follow.

Barb turned about so that she was facing back. "Now tell me why you can't go home," she said to the boy.

" 'Cause I was bad," he explained. "Broke a lamp. Monster going to get me."

"You were punished?" she asked. "For breaking a lamp?" Thor was concentrating on the escape, trying to direct Balook, but he was listening too. Barb was making progress with this incidental mystery. He had not known that she was good with children.

"Played too hard. It fell. Mom told me the monster would stomp me."

"The monster rhino?"

"Yes. Then I saw on the teevee the monster coming, so I went out to meet it."

"But why didn't you hide?" she asked.

"Didn't want it to hurt the house."

"You were afraid the monster would break down the house, just to get you?"

The child nodded.

"So you went out to meet it alone."

He nodded again.

"That was a very brave and generous thing you did, Fudgie!" she exclaimed.

"No, I was bad."

"Maybe so, but you paid for it. Now the monster is giving you a ride."

"A ride?"

"For being brave. The monster doesn't stomp brave children."

"It doesn't?"

"It doesn't. It's got better things to do."

The boy thought about that. Then, slowly, he smiled.

"I knew you'd understand," Barb said, hugging him. "Now you enjoy the ride, and look around, but don't fall off. Get a good hold, because sometimes it gets bumpy." She showed him how to hang on to the loose skin and hair, so as to be secure.

Then she oriented on Thor. "How are we doing?" She sounded grim.

"It occurs to me that we shouldn't let them know exactly where we're going," he said. "They'll be setting up roadblocks or worse. And if we get to the power company too soon, Mr. Turrell won't be there."

"So we need to hide for the night and some of the day," she said.

"Yes. But they can track us readily enough. I don't know if we can stay clear long enough."

"They won't close in too fast," she said.

"Why not?"

"Because we have a hostage."

"What?" Thor asked, shocked.

Fudgie took an interest. "What's a hostage?"

"It's a brave little boy who takes rides on monsters," she explained.

He liked that. "Is it 'portant?"

"Very important. Nobody can do anything until you finish your ride. Are you ready to go home yet?"

"No. I like riding."

"We'll let you ride with us as long as you want."

Thor realized that Barb had had reason to bring the boy along. The authorities would be helpless, because there was no safe way to get the boy down without the cooperation of the rhino, and Thor and Barb were the only ones who could guarantee that. They weren't really holding the child hostage, but his presence was exactly what they needed. They were already in so much trouble that a charge of kidnapping would not make much difference.

"What about the electromagnetic hazards?" Thor asked. "I have to know before I brace Mr. Turrell."

"How can something like that save Balook?" she demanded. "He's not a human being; he doesn't care about magnetic fields!"

"Precisely. What can you tell me?"

"All right," she said wearily. "Here is the short course; stop me when you get bored. The electromagnetic spectrum includes waves of all frequencies, ranging from X-rays down to ELF waves. Those aren't little men; that's an acronym standing for Extremely Low Frequency. Some waves are definitely dangerous to living things; some aren't. Microwaves affect a slew of things—I'd have to read my notes to remember them all—but there's genetic damage, loss of memory, cataracts, malformed fetuses—how much do you want?"

"What about power lines?" Thor asked.

"That's uncertain, but interesting. They generate the ELF. Fields of similar frequency are generated by the earth—the magnetic field—and the human brain. The theory is that when living things formed, they adopted the electrical environment, borrowing it from the earth, just as they adopted the nature of the sea water to make salty blood. So there's obviously a connection. If people are shielded from the earth's magnetic field, their biological cycles foul up. When the magnetic field reversed 25,000 years ago, several animal species became extinct; we don't know whether that's coincidence, but it's alarming. If it affected their brains—" She shrugged. "But of course most of the world's species, including ours, survived nicely. So we just don't know."

"What about the power lines? What do they do to people?"

"There isn't much information. The power companies have rallied to suppress studies, because there's no getting around the fact that civilization needs power. If we stopped the transmission of electricity, we'd be in a relatively primitive technological state, I think."

"But I've heard stories. C'mon, Barb, it's important!"

She sighed. "I certainly don't see how! Some experiments indicate that a strong ELF field near a human head induces anesthesia and affects the chemical balance in the brain, blood and liver. Bone tumors can occur. It may stunt growth. Bees in such a field can go crazy, sealing themselves up and dying. But it's inconclusive; other studies don't show these effects. So it's all one big question mark, and I can't tell you anything for sure."

"So the power lines generate ELF waves," Thor

said. "There's a lot of power in the air; you can light a fluorescent bulb without plugging it in."

"Yes; the power isn't just running through the wires; it's traveling a corridor thousands of meters in diameter, guided by the wire. But we normally can't even feel it. Thor, what is the *point*?"

"Would you take a full time job next to a power line?"

She laughed. "Not now! I don't know how much of the suspicion is true, but I wouldn't care to take the chance. I don't want my brain zonked out!"

"So how do you think the workers feel who have to stay close to those power lines?"

"Well, you know there aren't too many. Once the wires are connected, those lines are pretty much left alone. They use big clumsy machines to prune back the encroaching trees."

"Because they can't get enough human workers to do it!" Thor exclaimed triumphantly.

"I suppose. But I repeat: what is the—"

"Pruning back the trees," Thor said.

Then she caught on. "Oh, Thor, do you really think—?"

"We've got the world's best tree-pruners."

"But—"

"If I can just persuade the power company to hire them."

"But Balook can't prune anything if he's dead!" she cried.

He laughed humorlessly. "That had occurred to me."

"I think you're crazy!" she flared. "If the ELF is that bad for people, maybe, can it be good for Balook?"

"He was hours under those lines, and they never bothered him. It's a risk we'll have to take."

"I don't know. All this—this—"

He reached around Fudgie and caught her shoulders. He brought her face into him and kissed her. She met him warmly, then reconsidered and pulled back, then re-reconsidered and kissed him again.

"Gee," Fudgie said, wedged between them.

Barb tousled his hair. "I kissed him," she said. "Don't tell."

Fudgie knew about secrets. He agreed not to tell.

"There's something else," Barb said. "The Project—this publicity has been bad for it. The funds have been impounded."

"But the sale of the Western site—" Thor said.

"Yes, those funds. And an Act of Congress may shut down the Eastern site too. We may have nowhere to go."

"But the rhinos have to be somewhere!" he protested.

"Not if they are executed, because they have been judged a hindrance to the welfare of mankind." Now the reason for her grimness was clear. "That's why I broke them out, instead of just bringing you a rope. We're at the end of the line, no pun."

"They're going to hang the rhinos?" Fudgie asked.

"Same thing," Thor said. "They weren't really coming after you; they were fleeing from bad people."

"But they're *nice* monsters!" Fudgie said, beginning to cry.

"Yes, they are," Barb agreed, hugging him for comfort. But she was crying too.

Thor stared bleakly into the starry sky. Now his wild notion was truly their last resort!

THOR VERIFIED THAT cars were patrolling all the adjacent roads, and he was sure that all exits from the county were barricaded. But the authorities did not dare come into the forest after the rhinos during the night. So Barb took Fudgie to the ground to handle natural functions, then brought him back to be with Thor while she rejoined Theria. In the interim the little boy and the little rhino got together, seeming to like each other's company. Balook and Theria seemed not to notice; that was their way of signaling that they had decided that Fudgie was not a threat. In due course the human folk slept, while the rhinos browsed.

Then it was dawn, and two problems manifested. First, the three human beings were hungry. Second, there was a cordon around the area, impossible to pass unnoticed.

"Time to show our hostage," Thor said. "You understand what we're doing, Fudgie?"

"Making them leave us alone!" the boy said brightly.

"Yes. But we want your folks to know you are all right. You may stay with us until we talk to the man at the power company; then we'll all have to get down. I think by then your folks will have forgotten about the lamp. And after this, if a monster comes for you—"

"I'll pet it on the nose!" Fudgie said zestfully. His attitude about monsters had undergone a complete transformation during the night. He was enjoying himself now.

"Don't make us use force!"

They rode out to the highway.

"You are surrounded!" a speaker blared from a police car. "Don't make us use force!"

"What force?" Thor called back. "Do you want a dead rhino here? You can't do that until the appeal is denied." But he knew that that wasn't all of it. They did not want to shoot one rhino, and perhaps have Thor killed in the fall, and the other rhino go berserk and complicate things further.

"Wave to them, Fudgie!" Barb called from Theria.

Thor braced the lad with his hands, and the little boy stood up on Balook's six meter high shoulder and waved vigorously.

A ripple of dismay went through the assembled forces. Apparently they had not realized that the boy was with the rhinos. The stakes had abruptly risen.

"Now we want food and water," Barb called. "Delivered in standard containers, with no tricks."

"Donuts and chocolate milk!" Fudgie cried enthusiastically.

"Within the hour," Barb said. "I will come down for them. The others will remain on Balook. If anything goes wrong . . ."

It seemed to Thor that such a barefaced bluff could hardly work, but the men below were evidently daunted. They could not afford to have the hostage hurt—and they knew that if Balook got out of control, with the boy still on him, disaster was likely. It was an impasse, for the time being.

The supplies were brought. Barb collected them, took a share up to Thor and Fudgie, and then carried her own onto Theria.

"Now make way," Thor called. "We want a better pasture." He guided Balook slowly forward, and the men and cars got out of the way.

They crossed to the forest on the other side of the road. There was a scramble behind as the authorities sought to reform their cordon. But it hardly mattered, because the cordon was no longer a barrier to the party's passage. Thor let the rhinos forage, taking no particular direction, while the riders ate their own meal. It was like a picnic.

Then in midmorning he abruptly started the party moving. The men of the cordon were caught off guard as Balook forged purposefully to the highway. "Make way! Make way!" he cried.

"Make way!" Fudgie echoed gleefully. This was high adventure!

Now the rhinos proceeded down the road, directly toward the power station. Again there was a flurry of motion and much confusion as the authorities tried to reorganize. They were not apt at this; they had not even tried to negotiate. Thor had seized the initiative, and it stood him in good stead.

They made as if to pass the power complex—then abruptly veered into its open main gate. "Where's the president's office?" Thor demanded of the astonished attendant at the gate.

"Third floor, west side," the man said. "But you can't—"

"Thanks." Thor guided Balook to that portion of the main building. He saw amazed faces staring out of the windows.

He went to the fanciest window. "Push, Balook!" he directed. "Slowly!" Mostly he spoke with his foot signals, which the rhino understood better than the verbal ones.

Balook put his blunt nose to the window and shoved. The window broke inward, its plastiglass bending but not shattering. Then the frame collapsed, and a hole opened in the wall.

''Stay here, and hold on, Fudgie,'' Thor told the boy as he scrambled up on Balook's head. ''Hallo!'' he called into the window. ''Anybody home?''

There was a portly man at an ornate desk. ''This is an outrage!'' the man exclaimed.

Balook poked his head into the open window, carrying Thor along. ''Mr. Turrell, I presume? I must talk with you.''

''What on earth could you want with me?''

''Well, you wouldn't talk to me by phone, so I had to come in person,'' Thor explained. ''I really think what I have to say will be of interest to you.'' It had to be, or all was lost!

''This is preposterous!''

''I agree. But this whole situation can be relieved, if you will just give me a reasonable hearing.'' Thor was amazed at his seeming poise. It stemmed from desperation; he knew this was their only remaining chance, and he had to play it properly.

The man seemed ready to huff up until he exploded, but his voice was even. ''Suppose we talk for fifteen minutes? Will that satisfy you?''

''That's fine,'' Thor said, and slid off Balook's head. ''Go find a good tree, Balook,'' he said. ''But don't shake anyone off.'' He had already warned the boy about holding on; Fudgie had been delighted by the prospect of riding the monster solo. He had gone rapidly from terror to overconfidence.

''Now what do you think could be of such interest to me that you find it worthwhile to endanger the public, destroy property, and kidnap a child just to inform me about it?'' Turrell demanded.

"I want to save the life of a unique and innocent creature," Thor said evenly. "You want to make money. We may have a common interest."

"I want to serve the public interest," Turrell said angrily.

"That, too. So do I. I don't think that the public interest is well served by throwing away a billion dollar project without cause. Certainly it isn't by killing an animal who never tried to harm a man. Balook is no more guilty of manslaughter than is a car that slips its brakes and runs over someone who charges into its right of way."

"You may have a point, but that decision is neither yours nor mine to make. Exactly what are you getting at?"

"Suppose you had an efficient, reliable crew to prune back the vegetation that impinges on your power lines, that charged nothing for its services except maybe a drink of water every day?"

"Power transmission is a special problem," Turrell said. "We can't get reliable crews, so we use machines, inefficient and costly as they are."

"I know. But if a living crew offered to do it for nothing, and you knew that crew would never go on strike or leave for higher pay, what would it be worth to you?"

"I just told you: the matter is academic, because of the superstition against electromagnetic radiation. We have tried in vain to educate the public—"

"Just look out your window," Thor said. "See what my workers are doing to your trees."

Turrell looked. "Those animals are destroying those

trees!'' he exclaimed. ''At this rate—'' He broke off, astonished. ''You mean those rhinos?'' Suddenly the numbers were percolating through the man's head; he had a sharp eye for costs and savings.

''Put them in one of your power line corridors, install high electrified wires above the containing fences so the rhinos aren't tempted to stray, and they'll eat their way from one end to the other, leaving nothing within reach of the lines from a height of nine meters down. They don't require human guidance, except between corridors; they're a family. I think that pretty well covers your need. They could proceed right on to the neighboring power corridors, clearing them out too, and their manure fertilizing the grass below. It would be years before those trees encroach again, by which time—''

The door burst open. Armed men crowded in.

Turrel turned to face them. ''Can't you see we're having a private conversation?'' he snapped.

Abashed, the men retreated.

Turrell returned his attention to Thor. ''You were saying?''

''It would also be a nice public gesture,'' Thor continued. ''Most people like the rhinos; they just want them kept out of the way of human beings, so that nobody gets hurt. Your power corridors are private property, all fenced off. You could run pictures of the big rhinos doing this public service that human beings won't touch, and I think it would be pretty good publicity. The company with a heart, and a terrific mascot. And you would be helping science too, because—''

Turrell peered out the window. ''But the danger! They

trample children! We can't risk the liability suits if—''

He had broken off because Fudgie, perched on Balook's back, had grown too bold. Now the child was standing up and doing an impromptu dance, wowing his audience.

''Damn!'' Thor breathed. ''I told him to sit still and hold on!''

''He doesn't look like a captive.''

''He's not. He came to us voluntarily, because—'' Then Thor stopped. He had given away the secret of their hostage! Once the authorities knew that there was no threat to the child, they would have no reason to hold back.

''Get down, Fudgie!'' Barb called, alarmed.

Too late. The little boy lost his balance, teetered a moment, and fell. Screaming, he slid down Balook's side.

In a flash, Thor saw everything destroyed. A second injury to a child, or a second death—that would seal Balook's fate no matter what Mr. Turrell decided.

Then Balook brought his head about, surprisingly quickly. He caught the child on his big humped nose. The boy grabbed on automatically, though his body continued to slide down. But Balook's head was lowering toward the ground, and by the time the boy dropped off, he was only a meter from the turf. He landed screaming but unhurt.

''He saved that boy's life!'' Turrell exclaimed.

Thor realized that Balook had probably reacted to the sensation of the boy's slide down his side, and nosed him more from curiosity than aid. But he wasn't sure, because Balook had accepted the child as a rider, and did have a protective attitude toward those he accepted.

Blooky was there, nuzzling the crying boy. Fudgie reached up to hug the little rhino, taking comfort. People were gaping from the nearby parking lot. Light flashed. Some fool was taking pictures!

"Those rhinos are no danger to children!" Turrell said.

"Not when they see them coming," Thor agreed, immensely relieved.

Now Barb had dismounted and was with the child. It was all right.

"Young man, I believe we can deal," Turrell said. "I believe those pictures, and the testimony of witnesses, will satisfy the Mayor that a pardon is in order. I shall suggest that to him."

A pardon for Balook! There was the answer! The verdict of the judge could be set aside, and Balook would be free! But even as the joy of his success buoyed him, he felt the start of the great sadness of separation. Now neither he nor Barb would be needed; the *Baluchitheria* were to be self-employed.

But as he approached Barb, after having Balook rescue him from the office, he remembered his notion about the freak zoo.

"Balook and Theria and Blooky won't need us any more," he told her. "The power company is hiring them, and Balook will be pardoned. But there are other animals who do need us. We call it the freak zoo, and—"

"The freak zoo?"

"The failed experiments. I worked with them for two years while—" He shrugged. "There's Pooh, the miniature bear. He really needs a friend! Also Wormgear, the toothed worm. Nobody cares for them, because they aren't normal or pretty or smart. Even the regular personnel of the project really don't—''

''Are you suggesting that I join you there, to work with those creatures?''

''Well—'' he said, suddenly uncertain. He had assumed that she would want to, and to be with him, but of course that was a big assumption.

''Is there a lake there?'' she asked.

Then he knew it was all right.

AUTHOR'S NOTE

This short novel has a long history. It started with a picture in THE ILLUSTRATED LIBRARY OF THE NATURAL SCIENCES, a four-volume set of popularized geology, zoology, paleontology, botany and anthropology that has fascinating and not very complicated articles on just about anything in the natural realm. One article is titled Giant Animals, with pictures and commentary on the extremes of reptiles, mammals, birds, fish and such. The biggest reptiles were the dinosaurs; the biggest bird was the Elephant Bird, twelve feet to the top of the head, but of course it didn't fly; the biggest flying bird was an extinct vulture with a twelve foot wingspread. But this was dwarfed by the reptile Pteranodon, with a 27 foot wingspread. I am foolishly fascinated by such items. There was a drawing, made to scale, showing the extremes of mammals, with a six foot man for comparison. Dwarfing even the largest fossil elephant was *Baluchitherium*, whose head was about as long as the entire body of the man, and far more massive. Wow!

The thing that struck me about this drawing, upon reconsideration, was the pleasant expression on the face of the monster rhino. It looked as if it would be a nice creature to know. That nagged at me, because rhinos generally have a bad reputation. The truth, as another article explains, is that rhinos really aren't that mean when treated decently. So I formed this mental image of a really nice, huge rhino, who might be unfortunately misunderstood by ignorant folk of today. I carry such concepts around with me, and often that's as far as they go, just part of my private intellectual baggage, of no interest to sensible folk.

Then in 1966 *Data Processing Magazine* sponsored a contest: $1,000 first prize plus publication in the magazine, for the best computer fiction entry. Three of the six judges had done science fiction writing, so it seemed legitimate. As it happened, my wife was then a computer programmer, a ready source of information, so this contest seemed made to order for me. With her information and my writing skill—well, it seemed well within the realm of possibility that I could win it, and that would be very nice. All I needed to do was to write the story. I needed something interesting to go with the computer detail; what could I draw on? Well, suppose computers were used to help formulate some extinct species of animal? Perhaps an impressively large creature.

Thus "Balook" the 5,000 word story came to be. It featured Thor Nemmen, a computer programmer who worked with a computer system whose acronym was

BLOOK, and his introduction to a young woman who looked just like my wife and just happened to have a background in genetics (it's amazing how such coincidences occur!), and their project to recreate *Baluchitherium* with the help of computer technology. But it also had a moral. It started with a quote from Mathew Prior, *Solomon on the Vanity of the World*: "Who breathes must suffer, and who thinks must mourn; and he alone is blessed who ne'er was born." The opening was the yelp of a dog, to whose tail laughing boys had tied a string of cans, terrifying it. There was part of the theme: man's cruelty to animals. I am a vegetarian in part to protest such cruelty: the cruelty of killing animals for meat. Thus this story was close to home in several ways, for me.

They crafted Balook, intended to promote the capacities of the computer. But Balook was a living creature, and they had not properly allowed for his nature in the modern world. A mean man saw him and took a potshot (I don't much care for hunters, either), injuring him. Mean children laughed. That made them realize the enormity of the social problem. They had collaborated with a computer to play God, resurrecting an extinct animal. What price would Balook pay for their success? Had they really done more than tie tin cans on a living creature's tail? It concluded: "Had they forgotten the human responsibility man owed to the mechanical genius of the machine? Thor rested his arm against the guiltless nose of Balook, and was afraid." I felt it was a fine story, moral and all.

Indeed it must have been, because *Data Processing* held it nine months and returned it with a rejection slip.

That gives you a notion of computer efficiency in those days. My wife and I have made babies in no more time than that! The magazine published the winners of the contest, and I read the top three. You want sour grapes? I've got them in bunches! All three were poor. The first was essentially "I Love Lucy" cast in a computer framework, the computer running the household to the frustration of the occupants. The second was a power-failure problem whose author did not even know how to paragraph; it was all in big mixed-text blocks. (Didn't the editors know, either?) The third was better, as I recall, but unmemorable. Were I an editor, I would have bounced all three.

I tried it on the regular science fiction markets, hoping for more sensible reaction. There, at least, there was supposed to be some knowledge of literary and story values. The story bounced there too. But at least I got some comment—which is instructive in another fashion.

Anthony Cheetham of Sphere Books in England wrote: "Perhaps I have a more optimistic view of human nature than you do but I feel that the two small boys in the story would have been more likely to treat [Balook] as a favorite pet rather than stone him because of his size."

John W. Campbell of *Analog* wrote: "Sorry—the story doesn't seem to me to accomplish anything. Your hero might be pure ivory-tower-intellectual enough to be so naive as not to know what human beings are like—i.e., what the huge numbers on the lower slope of the distribution curve are like—but the heroine, as a psychologist-geneticist should have.

"Jack Schoenherr, our artist, who's an ardent and competent amateur zoologist, well known and respected at the Bronx Zoo, was in on the autopsy of a hippo that died there suddenly two years ago. The autopsy revealed that somebody had tossed it a can of lye.

"Must have made that guy feel real heroic to tear out the guts of a great big animal like that with a can of caustic.

"Zoos have trouble with flamingos too. They have bright pink knees in long, thin legs. Boys like to try to hit them with stones. It breaks the flamingo's leg."

This nicely demonstrates one of the problems writers have with editors: the same piece can be rejected for opposite reasons. Neither editor questioned the competence of the story; each bounced it because it did not conform to his ideological perspective for fiction. Not true enough to life—too true to life. I suspect we need less ideology in editing and more attention to straight story values. This was one of the reasons I finally left the story market and oriented almost wholly on novels. The book editors, while by no means perfect, were more tolerant of individual variance. Once I was able to express myself with less censorship, my career flourished. This, I think, is true for many writers: they have a better notion what the readers want than many editors do.

Obviously there are all types of people in the world. Some would make a pet of Balook; others would act exactly as I showed in the story. My point was not to establish or question the existence of such people; it was to show that *all* types have to be considered before an innocent but unusual creature is thrown among them. With the best of intentions, my characters committed a crime against nature—because they failed to consider the human environment Balook would face.

Ten editors found the story "Balook" unworthy. Did any of them understand it? I would say that Mr. Cheetham and Mr. Campbell came closest; both offered helpful commentary. I considered this commentary when I novelized it.

I, you see, am ornery. When I have what I deem to be a worthy notion, I am reluctant to accept rejection. When it became evident that the story magazines simply were not going to let Balook see the light of modern day, I set about trying it on the more liberal novel editors. I have done this with "Omnivore" and "A Piece of Cake" [TRIPLE DETENTE] and "Ghost" and others. I work relentlessly not only to write a good story, but to bring it to print. Sometimes it takes many years, even decades, but gradually I am catching up on the backlog. Now it is Balook's turn.

In 1967 I bought a British book, THE AGE OF MONSTERS by J. Augusta and Z. Burian, published by Paul Hamlyn of London. This had lovely pictures of the giants of the past. The seven foot tall *Diatryma* bird was the inspiration for the main character in my novel ORN. One picture showed a small herd of *Indricotherium*, the alternate name for Balook's species. Ah, joy! I set out to expand Balook into a family for the novel.

As part of this effort I set out to sculpt a statue of Balook. I am a prolific writer, and because of this some readers condemn my work on the grounds that it must be hack, ground out without regard to quality. These readers are ignorant of the nature of the writers of this genre. Science fiction and fantasy are among the most creative and exacting of the literary genres, and not the natural refuge of lazy or indifferent writers. I'm here because I love the genre; it alone allows me the latitude to explore my farthest notions. I have a wide spread of interests, and most of them can be accommodated here. I turn out a lot because writing is my way of life. Garden variety folk may relax by watching television or vacationing on the beach or dining in restaurants or simply snoozing on the couch; they want to forget their paying work. I can't blame them; I tried a number of mundane employments, and certainly these are well worth forgetting. My dream was to be a writer; to spend my time in the realms of farthest imagination, and to shape the products of my interests into stories that others would appreciate, so that I could thereby earn my living. Once that dream was realized, I remained wholeheartedly in it; who, upon entering Paradise, will turn about and return to mundane life? (Come to think of it, that could be why you don't see folk returning from Heaven after they die. Those in Hell have no choice, of course.) Thus I relax by reading things like THE AGE OF MONSTERS, and I turn on by writing about them, animating such creatures for my readers. I do whatever I need to do to make those creatures come alive. A man who did nothing but drink beer would consume a lot of beer; I do almost nothing but research and dream and write, and so I turn out a lot. None of it is careless or primarily for money. Money is a means, not an end.

I love Balook. I love writing. Anyone who reads this

novel and perceives only hackwork is welcome to return it for his money back; obviously he does not understand what I'm doing. Part of that love was expressed in the sculpture. It happened that at this time I met Sterling Lanier, another writer and a former editor—he was the one that fought to put Frank Herbert's novel DUNE into print after other editors rejected it because of its length, and he gave up editing when the resistance of publishers to such fine projects became too extreme. He's a fine writer in his own right. But few can earn a living exclusively by writing; he was also a sculptor. He carved fine little figures in wax and used the lost-wax process to have them rendered into metal statuettes. He had a fine spread of paleontologic representations, but none, I think, of *Baluchitherium.* He was active in the preservation of the environment. He also had a little girl the age of mine, and a wife the age of mine. In short, he was a good man.

Lanier showed me how to work with sculptor's wax, and I started in on Balook, pretty much as described in the novel. I had once aspired to be an artist, but gave it up in favor of words, the better medium for me. I had never really tried sculpting, but my dream of Balook hungered for more than words. I spend many hours on it, slowly shaping the figure from the wax while I wrote the novel. It was to be a huge statue for this process, six inches tall at the shoulder, and I hoped, if I could afford it, to have it cast in copper or silver, so that it could be with me relatively untarnished for all time. I can't justify this effort commercially; it was just something I had to do.

Meanwhile I marketed the novel on the basis of the

first two chapters and a summary of the remainder. It happened that I had met another writer at this time, Dave van Arnam, who showed me how to market this way. (Dave also had a little girl the age of mine. It is easy to relate to such folk.) I had been writing my novels entire, and the book editors were being almost as persnickety about submissions as the story editors. It was also a time of recession, and I was also being blacklisted by some publishers because I had started legal action against one in order to obtain royalties owed me. Thus I piled up eight unsold novels. Comments by another writer, Ted White, and Dave van Arnam showed me the error of my ways. By marketing on the basis of summaries, I could recover the leverage. If no publisher bought a project, I simply would not write it. That single change in marketing strategy tripled my income. I have been condemned by the ignorant for writing for money; I like to quote Samuel Johnson on that: "No man but a blockhead ever wrote except for money." I love to write, but if I don't get paid for it, I starve; *that's* why I now pay attention to the commercial side of it. You who condemn that—do you also condemn the plumbers and accountants and doctors and all the others who perform services for money? You think they should work for the love of it, unpaid?

So I marketed BALOOK from summary. But I was still new to this type of marketing, and a trifle uncertain. Suppose I got a contract, and a deadline for delivery—and then the novel didn't jell? So I kept on writing it. And a British editor liked it! He was ready to issue a contract, provided I did not have the characters refer to sex too specifically. Remember, this is a juvenile novel; teenagers may get pregnant and suffer venereal disease, but they may not read about sex. I agreed, and kept writing. Then the editor decided he'd rather see the whole novel first. Oh-oh; I had had experience with that sort of thing. "Not without a contract!" I said in essence to my agent. The publisher lost interest. I had seen it coming. I had almost completed writing the novel in pencil, but faced with this reneging, I halted work. Likewise the sculpture halted. I had to move on to other projects, because I had a family to support and money for writers is always close. I simply could not afford to put time into yet another unsold novel, however much I liked it. I had to cut my losses.

We tried the summary elsewhere, but editors seem to have a conspiracy: once one bounces a project, all the rest do. The novel, like the story, was moribund. Finally I retired it and the statue, both unfinished, with deep regret. The manuscript was secure in its folder, but my little girl had trouble understanding why I wouldn't let her play with the unused sculptor's wax. Then we moved, and parts got lost, and an ear got knocked off. The figurine was in a bad way. Today both front legs are missing, and one hind hoof; Balook can not stand, and his head rests separately beside his body. My dream of casting him in silver is ashes. Similarly, it seemed, I lost touch with Sterling Lanier; his marriage was in trouble and he had health problems. I looked at the battered Balook figure and I grieved for the misery it signified on every level. The thoughtless, unfeeling universe seemed the same outside the novel as inside it.

So it continued until the year 1986, twenty years after the story. My career had taken its twists and turns and abruptly leaped into high success via fantasy; I no longer had need to consider money when tackling a project. The blacklist was a thing of the past; I had survived it better than some of the blacklisting editors, which I think is simple justice. I was computerized, and zeroing in on word processing programs that served my needs with increasing accuracy. I had labored to place several of those eight unsold novels, and succeeded; only about three remained, and BALOOK, which didn't count because it had never been completed.

I entered a dialogue with a small publisher, Underwood-Miller, who was interested in publishing Anthony but of course unable to compete with the big outfits in terms of the large advances I now commanded. But as I trust I have made plain, money is not my overriding consideration. I suggested three projects that I might do simply because I liked the projects, money no object. One of them was BALOOK. This novel differed from some others in that I had a high visual involvement; I saw Balook, and wanted others to see him too. So we discussed artists, and I named the one I deem to be the best genre artist in the world, Patrick Woodroffe of England. The publisher agreed.

I mentioned word processing programs. I had discovered one called FinalWord that promised to be even better for me than my prior ones, and just had to try it, because in this as in writing itself I always try for the best. But it was complex, and not perfectly adapted to my system or my Dvorak keyboard; it would be a monster to break in. So I decided to use a story and a short novel to break it in; once I have novelized a thing, I really understand it. The story was "Imp to Nymph," which I retyped for the Program Book for the 1987 World Fantasy Convention. The available novel was BALOOK.

And so, at last, I returned to Balook, taking one month early in 1987 to complete it as I wrestled with the computer program, and this is the story of this illustrated novel. I hope that you, the reader, have enjoyed it—but even if you didn't, *I* did. Balook lives at last!